# Western Apprehension

## A Novel of the American Southwest

Written by

Michael Toled~~~

# *Forward*

Writing historical fiction requires more than just telling a story. It requires diligence on the part of the author to ensure that the main historical facts of the epoch are as accurate as possible. I've endeavored to maintain historical accuracy as far as my personal experience and research will allow. I have traveled through northeast New Mexico and have done extensive fact checking to be as accurate as possible. Where there has been uncertainty, such as what the locals at the time would call the poisonous mushrooms (Amanita pantherine), I've made my best educated guess.

Other details such as the history and culture of the Jicarilla Apaches, the models and accuracy of the different Winchester rifles, and how many miles a rider can travel in one day, etc. were methodically researched. Ancillary details proved rewarding and enlightening, such as the distance between towns on the Great Plains which were unofficially laid out to be a day ride from each other. Research may at times be grueling, but the bits of information you glean make it worth every bit of the effort.

I ask the reader's indulgence if there is a fact or two that I may have gotten wrong. I assure you that any such errors are a complete oversight on my part and the number of people that have critiqued my novel. Your feedback on any corrections would be most appreciated.

# *Chapter 1*

The pale light of early dawn signaled the next phase in the capture of the cornered fugitive. Dense woods circled a clearing where in the center stood a rustic log cabin. The clearing was surrounded by lawmen. Earlier, just before daybreak, U.S. Marshal Ben Corrigan had quietly positioned the posse around the perimeter. He and a couple of new, young marshals faced the front of the cabin. They used the fringe of the woods for cover. Next to the cabin was a small shelter where a couple of horses stood behind a crude wooden gate. In the growing daylight, Ben could see that one of the horses matched the description of the fugitive's mount, a dark chestnut with a white sock on its left hind leg. It shuffled around the shelter with a smaller black nag.

Clem Jordan was wanted for the murder of a fellow cowhand in a saloon brawl in Taos, New Mexico Territory. Ben had organized a posse in Taos shortly after the warrant for Clem's arrest was issued in early May of 1886. They tracked him for several days to the cabin in the Sangre de Cristo Mountains in the northeast part of the territory.

Two scraggly prospectors returning to their claim up in the mountains with fresh supplies from the nearby settlement of Red River had bumped into the posse. They told the Marshal that a woman lived alone in the cabin. They knew nothing about her. A previous attempt by the miners to approach the cabin to say "howdy" was met by "hell-fired" barking from her "rabid" dog and a warning blast of buckshot above their heads. From the looks of things, Clem was holed up with her. At this point, her status as a hostage or harborer was unknown.

The damp morning was clear and cold. Heavy dew soaked the foliage on the ground and everything else around the clearing. In the early daylight, the vegetation glistened. The chilled, moist air-filled Ben's nostrils. He occasionally shivered under his heavy leather jacket as he exhaled little, white puffs into the chilly air. From behind a sturdy pine, he had a clear view of the front door.

With enough daylight to proceed with the arrest, he pointed his rifle into the early morning sky and fired a piercing shot. As planned, a few members of the posse also fired booming shots into the air. From his secure vantage point, Ben stared at the cabin, waiting for a response. There was no return fire, no shouting, no screams, nothing.

"Clem…Clem, this is the law," Ben shouted toward the cabin. "We got you surrounded. You don't have a ghost of a chance of escapin', so you and the lady come out with your hands up."

An uneasy stillness followed Ben's demand. In the lull, he scanned the cabin, noticing more of its rough-hewn features in the growing daylight. Weather-beaten logs made up the dwelling's basic rectangular structure. It was topped by a roof of worn brown shingles. Each shingle was gnarled and twisted from years of relentless exposure to the sun, wind, snow, and rain. A short porch of warped gray floorboards led to a faded black door. The small windows facing the front had a brown film, and their frames had peeling white paint.

A flock of agitated blackbirds cackling overhead broke his gaze. He cleared his throat and yelled, "Clem, I'm only going to give you five more minutes to surrender. If you don't, I'll have no choice but to set fire to the cabin. It's over. Come out with the woman."

Still there was no response.

"You got less than five minutes before we torch the cabin. Now be sensible and give yourself up."

The seconds crawled into minutes. He remained upright, peering at the cabin from behind the thick pine. His young marshals were sprawled out next to him behind rocks they had piled up for protection. They had their rifles cocked, aimed, and ready to fire.

He checked his pocket watch. It was almost five minutes since he made his demand.
"Clem, time's up. You come out of there right now with your hands up, or we set fire the cabin. Do ya hear me?"

Several seconds went by with no response.

"He ain't gonna come out peaceable, is he, Ben?" asked Eddie Blake, one of the young marshals. Ben looked down at him. The youthful law officer was prone on the ground behind his shield of piled rocks. Eddie gripped his rifle, which was pointed at the cabin. The young marshal always had that touch of kindness that gravitated toward resolving any confrontation without the use of force. Ben wondered why a young man with such a mild disposition would want to choose a profession where violence was a common part of the job. But Eddie, at a muscular six feet five inches, could be intimidating, which he preferred to use over brute force.

He looked into the eyes of the apprehensive youth but gave no answer. Eddie stared back, searching Ben's face for any sign that the veteran marshal thought Clem would surrender without bloodshed.

Ben looked down, then at the cabin. "I reckon he's not. He knows he's gonna eventually hang if he surrenders. He may figure that being shot tryin' to escape is a lot better than being hanged." Ben heaved a sigh. "The trick is to make sure the woman and none of us gets hurt."

Everything was rapidly moving toward a violent confrontation. Ben tried to think of other bloodless options, but nothing came to mind. He scowled and muttered something to himself and then explained to Eddie, "There's nothin' else we can do. You and Whitmore light some torches. We'll have to set fire to the cabin. The flames and smoke should drive them out. I hope at least the woman comes out unharmed. Especially if she's being held, as I suspect, against her will. I sure hate the thought of harming her, but we've got no choice. If she's a hostage, then it'll only be worse for her the longer this thing drags on. If, by chance, she's in cahoots with Clem, it may take days before they surrender. Anything could happen, especially at night. Anyway, this posse is anxious to get home to their families. They'd never agree to waiting it out."

"Hey, Ben, the door's opening...it looks like someone's coming out," shouted George Whitmore, the other young marshal assigned to Ben. George had assumed a position directly to the left of Ben and Eddie. He, too, was prone on the ground behind a pile of rocks.

Eddie refocused on the open front door and joined George in training his rifle at the couple coming into view.

George Whitmore was the opposite of Eddie Blake in every way but height. His tall frame was slimmer and wirier. His dark eyes betrayed a sense of detachment from everyone's affairs but his own. A strong, angular face and upturned nose only accentuated his aloof disposition. Unlike Eddie, he was more inclined to use the raw power afforded by his badge to fulfill his duty.

The silhouette of a man clutching a woman by the waist and holding a gun to her head moved slowly from the open doorway onto the short porch. Ben and the young marshals sighted their weapons on the gunman. The members of the posse on the side of the cabin within view of the porch took fresh aim at the emerging figures. Those toward the back stood up and loosely pointed their rifles in the general direction of the cabin's front.

"You men, stay where you are and hold your fire," Ben shouted at the top of his voice.

"Clem, there's no cause to put this woman's life in danger. Let her go, drop your gun, and raise your hands. Haven't you done enough killin'? Let her be and surrender peaceable," Ben pleaded with the gunman.

"Surrender to what?" retorted an edgy Clem in a shrill voice, holding fast to the squirming woman with one arm while pressing his pistol to her head with the other. "A hanging because I killed a card cheat I caught red-handed who tried to go for my gun when I was walloping him with my bare fists?"

"That's not how I heard it from the witnesses," Ben shot back. "They say you gunned him down during the fight when he was clobbering you. He had no weapon, and the witnesses say they never saw him go for your gun. The plain truth is that you killed an unarmed man, and I'm charged with taking you into custody. Anyway, what's right or wrong about this business isn't for us to decide. It's up to the courts to hear you out and make a fair ruling. You'll have your chance to be heard before a judge and jury. It won't help if you add more charges to your record. Now let her be and drop your gun. It's over."

"I want my horse," Clem demanded. "Do ya hear me! And nobody followin' me. I'll let her go unharmed a few miles from here if you do as I say."

"You know I can't do that. What makes you think you'll still get away? Come on, Clem, it's over. Let her be and surrender now."

"I ain't gonna dance at the end of a rope for the amusement of a bunch of two-faced townspeople and their snot-nosed kids for trying to protect myself. That card cheat was gonna kill me with my gun I tell ya'. He was goin' for my gun to kill me! I had to protect myself. Now I ain't got nothin' else to say. Someone get me my horse!"

Ben let out a long sigh, but before he spoke again, the woman shrieked, dropped her head, and lunged her shoulders forward despite Clem's tight grip on her waist. For a split second, everyone froze. Then there was the blast from a gunshot on Ben's left. As Ben flinched, he saw Clem thrust backward, flinging his arms out and, in the process, throwing his pistol several feet in front of the porch. Clem's body bounced off the cabin below the high windows before hitting the floorboards on the porch. The woman, freed from Clem's grip, fell to the ground in front of the cabin. She lay there sobbing while Clem lay motionless, facedown and spread-eagle. A part of the top of his skull was missing, and blood was pouring from the gaping wound.

The other members of the posse came running toward Clem and the woman. A few of them tried to console her while the rest hovered over Clem's lifeless body.

Ben looked to his left to see Eddie Blake, with his eyes and mouth wide open, staring at a grinning George Whitmore, who was holding his smoking rifle.

"Nice shootin', son," Ben said sarcastically. "Good thing you knew you wouldn't hit the woman."

"No, sir," replied George. "No cause for concern because I had a clear enough shot at him once she ducked. I knew I couldn't mistakenly hit her. Otherwise, I plumb wouldn't have taken that shot."

Ben's scowl melted into a trace of a smile. He walked toward the cabin and approached the woman, who was now standing with the help of two men from the posse. They held each of her arms in an effort to steady her and were gently speaking words of comfort. Tears flooded down her pretty, ivory-complexioned face and onto an ample bosom. A clean, blue calico dress draped her full figure, and she wore black buttoned shoes polished to a high luster. Her dark brown hair was coiffured into the fashionable wave that wrapped neatly around her head. Everything about her spoke of refinement, creating a curious juxtaposition with the coarse cowhand, Clem Jordan, and her crude dwelling.

"Howdy, ma'am," Ben softly greeted her. "Are you hurt?"

The woman looked at him with bleary eyes as she tried to control her crying.

"Ma'am, are you okay?"

When she tried to speak, she could only splutter. In an effort to respond she nodded, acknowledging that she was unharmed.

Ben turned to both men propping her up and asked, "Has she said anything?"

"No, she ain't uttered a word," answered a short, heavyset man with a thick-bearded face. He was the one holding her right arm.

"She's all shook up, poor soul. It may take her a quite a spell before she calms down, considering all she's been through," said the other man, a rotund fellow with a handle bar moustache who was holding her left arm.

Ben glanced back at the woman. A strong feeling of compassion swept through him. "You men take her back to the cabin and get her a cup of coffee. I'll check with you later." He bowed to the distressed woman and said, "Ma'am, I'm awful sorry. Please find a way to get a hold of yourself. I'll need to ask you some questions before we head back to Red River."

Ben headed toward the corpse on the porch as the two men led the distraught woman toward the cabin door. He stepped onto the porch with trepidation and was clearly disturbed by what he saw. What was left of the top of Clem's head made him wince. Blood oozed from the missing scalp, and some brain matter was splattered above Clem's skull. Clem's arms and legs were stretched out and his face was pressed against the boards, which, for now, spared Ben and the others from seeing his death grimace.

Ben looked at all the men congregating over the grisly sight. Their stunned expressions revealed how shocked they were at the gruesome spectacle.

"Quite a nasty mess," mentioned one of the men staring at the corpse. "I've never seen anything like this since I was in the Battle of Cold Harbor."

"I've been on posses before," said another man in the group. He spat out some of his chewing tobacco and shook his head. "I don't ever recollect seeing something so dang disgusting."

"Ain't a pretty picture, is it?" Ben asked rhetorically. "In all my years as marshal, I've seen more than my share of these God-awful shootings when they won't surrender peacefully. I never got used to them."

"What do you want us to do with him?" another man in the group asked Ben.

"Someone find a horse blanket in the shelter or in the cabin. Wrap him up and tie him across his horse. He's supposed to be riding the chestnut quarter horse with a Circle W brand on the hindquarters. We'll take him to the undertaker in Red River. After that, you men can go home. I got all your names. The territorial governor will pay you for your services, just as we agreed."

He went to the open doorway leading into the cabin in search of the woman. He entered the single room, which was dimly lit by candles and daylight coming from the small, high windows facing the front porch. A small fire in the fireplace greeted him with a welcome warmth after the chill outside. The pleasant aroma of coffee filled the air. Apparently, the coffee had already been brewing before Ben ordered Clem to surrender. The room was clean and cozy, with a spinning wheel in the corner to the right and a bed with a green plaid quilt in the corner to the left. There were baskets placed everywhere with fruit, flour, and other household items. All these were neatly arranged over an unpolished wooden floor worn smooth by years of foot traffic and the sweeps of many brooms like the one by the doorway. All the walls had hanging shelves filled with cooking utensils, jars, glasses, knick-knacks, and books. Many hats and some clothes were also hung on the walls nearest the bed. Mounted on the wall to the left of the bed was a double-barreled shotgun.

At the farthest corner from the door there was a small table with a red-and-white checkerboard tablecloth and a single chair where the woman was quietly seated. She had a steaming cup of coffee in front of her. Her eyes were closed and her head tilted downward on slumped shoulders. She sat with her hands in her lap facing in the direction of the Marshal. One of the men who had accompanied her into the cabin was standing near her sipping coffee with his foot on a stool by the table. The other man was placing the coffee pot on the small grill made for a coffee pot that was off to one side in the fireplace.
Ben looked at one and then the other, seeking from their expression to discover whether they had made any progress in communicating with her. Both shook their heads—no.

"Ma'am, as painful a time as this may be, I need to ask you some questions."

The woman lifted her head, opened her swollen eyes, and stared at Ben. He noticed that the left side of her face had a reddish bruise.

"Can you tell me your name?"

"Jenny...Jenny Carpenter," she said firmly but in a whisper.

"Well, that's a promising start. Do you know Clem Jordan?" Ben asked, as civil as he could.

"Yes, but I hadn't seen him in months since we broke up over his drinking and his bad temper," she answered defensively in a clear, raised voice. "Yesterday, he knocked at my door. I was so surprised. He pleaded with me to let him in because he needed my help. He sounded terribly upset. I could tell he was scared. He begged me to let him in. When I opened the door, he shoved his way inside."

"Why do ya think he came here?"

"I swear, I don't know." Her voice was still raised and trembling.

"What do you do around here?" Ben continued to prod.

Jenny lifted her head and wiped her eyes with the back of her hands. She answered Ben in a hushed voice. "I'm the school teacher in Red River."

"And you live here alone?" Ben asked with a touch of surprise.

"Yes, I've been widowed these past ten years. My husband died at the Little Bighorn in June of '76. Up until now, I've always felt quite safe. Red River is just over the hill. I'm good with a shotgun, and I had a big dog to warn me until he disappeared a few weeks ago."

Ben looked about the room with approval at how kempt it was. "Is this your cabin?" he asked casually.

"No, I'm renting it from Eugene Caruthers, the blacksmith in Red River."

"I see. You said Clem forced his way into the cabin. What happened afterwards?"

"He told me he needed to hide out for a few days because he killed a man in self- defense, but nobody believed him, and a posse was closing in on him." Jenny looked up at Ben, pleading with him to believe her. "I told him I didn't want to get mixed up in any part of this and for him to get out. When he refused, I tried pushing him out the door. He ...he started hitting me. I tried to fight back, but he was much stronger than me." Her voice rose and became shaky. "He tied me up. ... I screamed at him. ... He gagged me. ... I was tied up all night until you hollered at him to surrender. That's when he untied me and forced me to go with him out the door."

"Thank you, ma'am. I'm truly sorry for what happened. We'll need you to come with us into town to file a written report. After that, you're free to go. Is there a close friend in town that you can stay with overnight? I think it's best for you not to be alone."

"Yes, there's Amy Fletcher, my best friend. She and her husband won't mind taking me in for the evening. Anyway, I really don't want to stay here tonight. I just couldn't."

Ben looked at both men and said, "Help her saddle her horse." He tipped his hat and headed out the door.

"Clem's body's wrapped and tied to his horse," George said to Ben.

"How's the woman?" asked Eddie.

"She's out of sorts, but she'll survive," Ben replied, trying to ignore the fresh images of the distraught schoolteacher. "Okay, let's mount up and get going," Ben called out to everyone.

As they all mounted their horses and waited for a few of the men to saddle Jenny's horse, he silently asked himself how much longer he wanted to deal with these kinds of situations. His partner in romance, the widow Rachel Langford, had asked him the same question. She wanted him to retire his badge and settle down with her, closing out a long, successful career of surviving all manner of life-and-death confrontations. Yet despite his job's travails, he couldn't imagine waking up every day to life in a rocking chair and not a saddle.

# *Chapter 2*

The clock chimed eight o'clock. From behind his desk, Deputy Slim Colson put down his coffee mug, gave out a big yawn, and stretched his arms. He cleared his throat and stared at the clock to be sure it was time to begin his evening patrol down Main Street. A genial man, he enjoyed his position as the second-ranking peace officer in the dusty town of Iron Horse Junction, located at the southwest edge of the Great Plains. Together with the equally affable Sheriff Willy Gibson, they enforced the statutes on the books and encountered little more than a few misdemeanors that rarely required the use of force.

Truly blessed, he liked his job, adored his pretty wife, and loved his five lively kids. The perfect father, the tall skinny deputy doted on his family when he wasn't on duty. Known for taking his husbandly and fatherly duties seriously, he also cultivated friendships with everyone in town. No one could recall anyone saying a bad word about him. Even when administering his official duties, he did so with firmness that had the utmost of civility.

When the chimes stopped, Slim folded his arms and took a deep breath, content to linger for a few more seconds in the comfort of his chair. The incessant tick tock from the shiny brass wall clock pestered him to get on with his rounds. Reluctantly, he stood up, pulled down on his ten-gallon hat, adjusted the gun holster slung at an angle around his waist, heaved a sigh, and headed out the door into the bright but waning sunlight of a clear mid-May evening. The square-jawed Slim used to enjoy his evening jaunt exchanging greetings and good-natured barbs with the townspeople he knew and liked very much. That was before an unruly stranger came into town a few weeks ago, making a nuisance of himself most nights at the Arroyo Saloon.

The drifter's name was Frank Jameson. He was followed by two pals shortly after being hired as a cowhand at the Bar-Z Ranch just outside of town. His two friends joined him herding the cattle at the Bar-Z. They were just as ornery as Frank and looked up to him as their ring leader. Together they made up a trio of rowdies the likes of which the townspeople had never seen before. Frank, a tall, hefty man, had enormous arms and chest. He was physically intimidating. His face was ruddy, pockmarked, unshaven, and accentuated by a disfigured nose that looked like it had been broken several times. He rode into town three or four evenings a week to frequent the Arroyo Saloon with his rough-hewn friends, who also bore scars on their stubbly faces.

Inevitably, all three made a nuisance of themselves as the night wore on and the drinking took its toll. Boisterous, they would laugh and talk so loud that everyone took notice of them. Frank enjoyed being the center of attention.

Many times, late into the evening, Frank or either one of his two friends would get especially ill-tempered and hurl insults and challenges to anyone within range of their table.

During their time at the saloon, the bartenders worked as a team to hold the troublemakers in check. They would only call the sheriff or the deputy if they couldn't get them to settle down. Throughout the night, the saloon keeper warned the rowdies to mind their behavior or they would be told to leave. After voicing vulgar protests of innocence, Frank and his friends would laugh it off and temporarily restrain themselves only to build up to another bout of loud misbehavior. When it was finally closing time, the saloon staff promptly ushered Jameson and his pals out the door, bearing the drunken insults and expletives with relief. They often discussed barring the three from the saloon, but they wondered whether it would cause more trouble than it was worth. They simply hoped that the three miscreants would finally take the strong hint from the saloon's staff that they were unwelcome. Since this was the only watering hole in town, it was a slender hope.

Nevertheless, the sheriff and Slim decided that they had had enough. One more disorderly incident from the Jameson gang, and they would throw the troublemakers out of town and bar them from entering the city limits under penalty of arrest. Slim was hoping that he wouldn't have to enforce this decision any time soon. Maybe Jameson and company would finish their work at the Bar-Z and move on. But after talking to the disagreeable Hank McCutcheon, the owner of the Bar-Z, Slim knew it was unlikely Jameson and his buddies would be leaving soon. Hank didn't much care for the three of them, but they were a "hell of a gang of cowpunchers" and worked for cheap wages. It seemed that room and board and the Arroyo Saloon were all that they needed. The money they earned they spent on the liquor, the female companions for hire, and the gambling at the Arroyo.

As much as he hoped it wouldn't happen, Slim knew the day of reckoning would come. Jameson and his friends would continue their raucous behavior, forcing the law officers to enforce their decree. So when a frantic Ted Neely came running down the street yelling the deputy's name, Slim's instincts told him the time had come.

"Deputy Slim...Deputy Slim...come quick...something mighty awful has happened," an out-of-breath, short man with a distinctive black bowler shouted at Slim. The man wore a rumpled black suit and had a lopsided black string bow tie that unmistakably identified him as the town's undertaker.

"Why, Ted, what's the matter? Your wife threatening you with a frying pan 'cuz you gambled away the family cow?" Slim asked with a smile and a thick drawl, hoping that it was some other matter that had caused Ted to be in such a state.

Ted abruptly stopped in front of Slim. He doubled over, resting his hands on his knees, staring at the ground trying to catch his breath. His round, full face was red, and his forehead was drenched in sweat. "No, sir, ain't nothin' as trivial as that. Besides we ain't got no cow. It's Jameson at the Arroyo. He's done beat out the brains of that cattle buyer from Omaha with the leg of a chair he broke over the man's head."

Slim's smile melted into a stern gaze as he stared in the direction of the Arroyo at the far end of Main Street. He inhaled and exhaled slowly, wrinkled his brow, and walked directly toward the saloon. "That so.... Got to be," the deputy mumbled.

"Deputy Slim, be careful, Jameson's gone loco and he's plumb drunk as a skunk."

Slim turned his head toward Ted Neely while walking briskly towards the saloon, "Go fetch the sheriff."

"Yes, sir, I'll go directly." Ted took a deep breath and ran in the direction of Sheriff Gibson's home on the outskirts of town, in the opposite direction of the saloon.

*Francis Benham Jameson was born on a chilly late-November day to a prostitute in the backroom of the brothel where she worked. Francis was the woman's father's name. Benham was her mother's maiden name. Jameson was the clan. Nothing is known of Frank's father, except that he was undoubtedly one of his mother's unnamed customers. It could have been anyone from the nearby army post or the group of female-starved cowboys that came into the central Kansas town at the end of a long cattle drive. It may even have been one of the respectable churchgoing town residents.*

*Hester Angela Jameson was his mother's name. She was the sole survivor of an Irish immigrant family who perished during an Indian raid on their miserable frontier homestead during one of the many Indian uprisings protesting the white man's encroachment. Within a terrifying few minutes, her parents, three older brothers, a younger sister and brother, and a baby sister were brutally killed. The fifteen-year-old Hester was found by the raiding party in a corner of the family's sod shack. She was crying hysterically while clutching the bloody remains of her dead baby sister. Hester's life was spared because the head of the raiding party wanted her. He ripped the dead infant from her arms and dragged her by the hair to his pony. Then he knocked her unconscious, tossed her limp body over the withers of the pony, and carried her away to his village.*

*Hester lived there for two years and had borne the Indian brave two daughters. When she was finally released as part of a treaty that returned all white captives, she wasn't allowed to bring her half-breed children with her into the white man's world. An undesirable misfit despoiled by savages, the lonely Hester drifted into prostitution as the only means of survival.*

*Francis Benham Jameson was made an orphan at the age of six when his mother was killed during a dispute between two soldiers who argued as to which one was going to sleep with her. At the time, Frank was living and doing chores to earn his keep with a saloon keeper's family. During the fracas, as his mother was trying to restore peace, one of the soldier's revolvers accidentally discharged, striking Hester in the heart and killing her instantly.*

*Frank's fate, naturally, was put in the hands of the owner of the saloon, Zeke Arneaux. Zeke was a bad-tempered, often-drunken brute who mistreated his family and especially the young Frank. Never a day went by that Zeke didn't inflict some physical and verbal abuse on the boy. Zeke's family was indifferent to Frank, and they were relieved when Zeke heaped abuse upon him instead of them. Nurtured by this brutal upbringing, Frank's turbulent nature took form. He, in turn, became a hell-bent bully, always up to no good and spoiling for a fight. So, when the sixteen-year-old Frank turned on Zeke and beat him senseless during one of their daily altercations, it set the stage for Frank's future. Frank fled and wandered aimlessly through the Southwest, creating trouble wherever he went.*

Slim could hear the commotion as he approached the saloon. A number of loud voices raised in anger blared into the street from inside the Arroyo; the loudest coming from the dissonant, gruff voice of Frank Jameson.

"Anybody else wanna make trouble for me! I'll...I'll...knock off all your heads, you bastards!" a fired-up Jameson bellowed.

Slim entered the saloon through the faded green double doors. The strong smell of whiskey and tobacco smoke hung in the air. A number of people were standing and staring at the commotion in the center of the saloon, where Jameson stood amid tossed tables and chairs, brandishing a thick wooden chair leg glistening with fresh blood at the male patrons and bartenders that surrounded him.

A few of the patrons had overpowered his two pals, pinning them to the floor. The mix of men around Jameson were tightening the circle, backing away when Frank lunged at them but jumping back into position when Frank turned to face another. On the floor near the bar, a man in a pinstripe business suit lay sprawled on his back next to a mangled chair missing a leg. The top of the man's head was split open. He wasn't moving, just bleeding profusely from the head wound. One of the satin-clad bar girls was on her knees next to the body, crying inconsolably while another with a yellow feather in her hair stood rubbing the kneeling girl's shoulder trying to comfort her.

When everyone noticed Slim, the circle opened in his direction. Erect, motionless, hands by his side, he sternly faced Jameson. Slim wanted to draw his pistol, but he noticed Jameson was also holstering a gun. He didn't want to risk a gun battle in the crowded saloon.

"Okay, Frank. Put it down. We don't want no more trouble."

Jameson glared at Slim with blurry, red eyes filled with rage.

"Frank, drop it. …Now. …and raise your hands. You're under arrest."

Jameson stood frozen, clutching the bloody chair leg and pointing it at Slim. He stared a hole through Slim. Then his scowl melted into a smile.

"Aw'right, Deputy. I'll come peaceable. It ain't my fault. This city slicker was spoilin' for a fight. He came at me first. I swear." The saloon erupted into a murmur of protest but became silent when Jameson dropped the chair leg and raised his hands.

Slim relaxed and walked toward Jameson. The men around Jameson gave way and allowed him to move toward Slim—toward being arrested. As Slim took his eyes off Jameson and turned his attention to reaching for the handcuffs near his holster, Jameson dropped his right arm, quickly drew his gun, and fired a shot at Slim. Slim flinched and gaped silently at the blood spewing from his chest, then collapsed to the floor. A couple of the bar girls screamed, and men roared curses at Frank.

The men around Jameson pounced on him, knocking the gun from his hand. They piled on top of him, holding him fast.

"He's dead," a man checking Slim's pulse at his wrist announced.

At that moment, Ted Neely and Sherriff Willy Gibson entered the saloon.

# *Chapter 3*

They were in the parlor of Rachel's home, in the town of Millbrook, facing each other from opposite ends of the room. Time slowed to a crawl. Ben welcomed his neutral corner. He could tell that Rachel disliked the distance between them. Even though her hands were already dry after cleaning the dishes, she continued to rub them on the dish towel. Through the open curtained windows facing Main Street, the town's early-morning activity unfolded: children with their school books running and shouting, a few wagons loaded with goods creaking in the street ruts, chattering women with baskets heading towards the country store, men on horseback swaying while their mounts rhythmically clopped down the street.

The little room was comfortably furnished with a plush beige sofa and a shiny brown-leather love seat that took up most of the space. The polished wooden floor spoke measures of Rachel's tidy nature. Its high gloss shimmered even in the faint early-morning light that crept into the room. A few pictures of varying landscapes were placed with care between oil lamp fixtures that accentuated the smooth, almond-colored walls. The lingering smell of a recently cooked country breakfast hung in the air.

"Rachel, I can't stay any longer to talk about this," Ben said, trying to reason with her. "I gotta leave and fetch the prisoner from Iron Horse Junction and bring him to Santa Fe for trial. There's just so much to think about. We'll have to finish talking about this when I return."

"You said you wanted to marry me," Rachel declared, searching his face for assurance. "Have you changed your mind?"

"This is not the right time," he stated. "I'm not sure I'm ready to give up my job just yet. You know I can't be tied down while I'm a territorial marshal. At times, my job is so dangerous, and I'm away from home for such long spells. …I don't want to give you the same heartache I gave Nora. I just can't do that, and I don't ever want to leave you a widow for a second time."

"I'm not like my sister Nora, God forgive her. I could never do what she did to you."

"I know. I know. But it's not my only concern."

Rachel lowered her voice just above a whisper. "Look, we've talked about this more times than I'm willing to count. When do we move on with our lives…together?"

He looked at the window and stared at the commotion outside on the small town's dirt-packed Main Street.

"Then you really don't love me," Rachel said pointedly.

"You know that isn't true," he protested.

A tear stole down her cheek. "Then last night and all the nights we've spent together have been...."

"Rachel, please," Ben shot back. "You know that's not so. For heaven's sake, your womanly instincts should tell you that."

"I want to hear it from you. Do you love me?"

"Of course, I love you." Ben moved toward Rachel, looking into her eyes and beyond. He put his arms around her and kissed her.

She responded with equal fervor. While locked in their tight embrace, Ben could feel the ardor of her kiss and the warmth of her breath. Her body, clasped tightly to his, radiated with her desire, her sensuality, her intensity, her love. It never failed to overwhelm him. It was the prelude to the inevitable higher pitch of lovemaking—but not this time. Faced with the impact of ending a career that was a way of life for him since his budding youth, Ben found the dilemma overrode any further affectionate urge. He cringed when he thought of the compromise of continuing his career and being married to Rachel. The ruin of his past marriage to Nora, created by his long absences, haunted him. It was a relentless specter that interfered in making the ultimate union with Rachel.

Ben whispered, "Please, you gotta understand. It's hard for me to get over my past and not worry about hurting you. Lord almighty, it would tear me to pieces if I harmed you in any way."

Rachel broke free of his embrace, placed her hands on his shoulders, and looked him straight in the eyes. "You must let me know soon. I can't go on much longer like this. Whether you realize it or not, you're hurting me. I love you, but I can't wait forever. If you can't make a commitment, then our lives must move on."

Ben returned to looking out the window. The thought of settling down with Rachel seemed so right but at the same time so discomforting.

"Let me finish this job. I'll come back to you as soon as I can. We'll talk again. We can decide how we are going to plan our future. If you can't wait until then, I understand. I don't want to mislead you or cause you any further heartaches. It wouldn't be fair. It wouldn't be right."

An uneasy truce pervaded the silence between Ben and Rachel as he hastened to gather his belongings and leave. For the first time since their relationship became serious, he felt awkward and unsure what to say. She avoided any direct eye contact and remained stoic while helping him pack.

She helped Ben take his belongings to the large wooden stable out back. A handsome one-story, dark-red structure with decorative beige accents, it was as prim as her well-kept home. The building had plenty of space for her horse and buggy and a few extra stalls for the transport animals of visitors, which most times were her sons' carriage horses when they brought their families to spend time with Ma—Grandma.

When they had finished stowing his gear on the pack mule, he saddled his horse. Ben turned to say some soothing words in parting. Rachel preempted him. She made quick turns of her head to make sure that they were beyond prying eyes and pecked a kiss on his cheek. As she swiftly walked away, she said, "Please be careful. ...I'll be waiting for you." Then she disappeared into the house.

Taking one long last look at Rachel's cozy, white house, he mounted his horse and led his pack mule toward the southwest, out of the little windblown town. He wondered whether Rachel really understood his concern and apprehension, and if indeed she would be waiting for him.

# Chapter 4

Rachel rushed into the kitchen through the back door and quietly closed it. The departing hoofbeats of Ben's horse and mule had long faded into the distance. Drained and despondent, she didn't want to move. Leaning against the door became a temporary sanctuary. She spent several minutes with her eyes closed. This thorny love affair tested her mettle in ways that went beyond any previous torment. Who would have imagined her falling in love with her sister's widower? The consequences created more turmoil in her life than she had ever imagined.

Ben loved her. She was certain of it. But if he loved her as much as she loved him, then why couldn't he make the commitment? Was this a wasted romantic venture in the twilight of her life? If so, then why hadn't her mature instincts prevented such a disaster? Of all the suitors since her husband's death almost nine years past, Ben was the only one with whom she had found honest consolation and real love. No others came close.

She opened her eyes and pulled on the ribbon of her sunbonnet, loosening the knot. Pursing her lips, she tried to clear her mind, making a desperate attempt to plunge into detached sensibility. She was the proud mother of two grown boys who lived nearby. They had exceptional wives. They had made her the grandmother of five beautiful grandchildren: three from George and two from Harry. Both their families were coming to stay this weekend. She had much to do. While hanging the sunbonnet on one of the pegs on the wall, she uttered a quick prayer for Ben. Then she grabbed the broom and began sweeping the kitchen floor. The reality that her life must move on with or *without* Ben flashed through her mind. Dropping the broom, she covered her face with her hands. Before the broom handle hit the floor with a clack, the kitchen walls echoed with her sobs.

\*     \*     \*

The next day, after a restless night, Rachel headed to the general store. Her day usually began with a number of chores. Today, because of the expected company, a few extra errands would be added to her list. As she walked with her basket, her pretty, expressionless face caught the attention of Kristoffer Svendsen, the town banker who was walking in the opposite direction to his office at the bank.

Shortly after her husband's death, Kristoffer wooed Rachel with all the persuasion he could muster. Rachel's husband, Henry Langford, had been one of the town's prominent citizens. He was a successful land speculator before he was killed in a tragic carriage accident while surveying a prime acreage put up for sale just outside of town. Henry left Rachel a modest fortune. He was the largest depositor in the town's only bank, owned by Kristoffer. With Kristoffer's financial advice, she would live comfortably the rest of her life. Rachel and Kristoffer had spent many long hours reviewing her deceased husband's estate—to his delight. Unfortunately, this brought them in contact with Fred Winkelman, the town's well-educated attorney. Fred also had designs on Rachel and her fortune.

Once both realized that Rachel's love interest lay firmly elsewhere, Fred abandoned his effort and decided to stay with his wife and children. However, for Kristoffer, it was a blow from which he was slow to recover. He remained a bachelor, watching with regret as Rachel's two young sons grew into manhood without his guidance and with envy as Ben made the conquest he thought he deserved.

"Rachel, my dear, how are you this fine morning?" Kristoffer asked with a trace of a Norwegian accent. He stopped and doffed his hat. Kristoffer was a big man with large hands that made his brown derby look smaller than it was when he held it by the narrow brim. His youthful head of blond hair had given way to a bald pate circled by a thick crop of gray hair. Well into middle age, he looked remarkably fit in his six-foot-four-inch frame. In his younger days, he was a professional prize fighter of some repute. The scars on his round face and offset nose gave testimony to his former profession. Nonetheless, he was ruggedly handsome, and many a woman had taken notice.

He left the boxing ring and its tawdry grind when an unexpected business opportunity presented itself. With the money he diligently saved, he and a few partners rescued a failing bank in St. Louis. Over time, he learned the business, sold his share in the bank, went West looking for bigger prospects as a sole proprietor, and opened Millbrook's first financial institution. The town's only bank flourished. He thrived in its success.

"Good morning, Mr. Svendsen. Yes, it is a fine morning, and I'm doing quite well. Thank you," Rachel responded cordially, but with unmistakable detachment.

"May I ask how are your two boys and their families?"

"They are doing as well as expected. They're to visit me this weekend. I'm so looking forward to seeing them, their wives, and my grandchildren."

"Ah, you've certainly been blessed with a wonderful family. Mr. Langford, I'm sure, is looking down with great pride."

Rachel recoiled but kept her composure. Kristoffer usually brought a reference to her husband's celestial presence into their conversations. Until recently, she thought that it was Kristoffer's way of making a favorable impression. Lately, it took on the veiled overtone of an admonition of what

Henry's spirit would say about her well-known, torrid, unabashed romance with her sister's widower.

"Yes, we have. Well, it's good to see you, Mr. Svendsen. Do have a nice day."

Before Kristoffer could reply, she hurried on her way, leaving him to stare longingly at his ideal of a *grande dame* once more slipping away. With a sigh, he put on his hat and continued walking toward the bank.

# *Chapter 5*

Sheriff Willy Gibson heaved a long sigh as he continued his futile attempt to ignore the commotion outside his office. He sat upright in his sturdy oak chair with his feet propped atop a solid wooden desk. His powerful arms were crossed and rested on his ample stomach. Under a wide-brimmed, white hat, he stared absently at his finely etched boots. The crowd outside had gathered immediately after the services for his partner and best friend, Deputy Slim Colson. They alternated between singing spiritual hymns and making speeches in eulogy for the gunned-down deputy. Still recovering from the brutal slayings of his partner and a traveling cattle buyer from Omaha, Willy was further troubled by being the custodian of Slim's murderer in a jail cell in the back room. Oh, how he wanted to mete out swift frontier justice. But he swore an oath to uphold the law. That, and the ultimate satisfaction that Frank Jameson would certainly hang, held him in check.

As the afternoon progressed into evening, the throng became more restless. Increasingly, people shouted demands, urging the sheriff to release the prisoner to the townspeople for punishment. He mused that if he weren't wearing the badge, he would be out there making the same request. An additional burden of uneasiness weighed on him as he wondered whether the gathering of his respected neighbors and close-knit friends would degenerate into a lynch mob.

Where was his newly deputized nephew, Nathan, and that one-eyed handyman, Lester, also sworn in as a deputy? Nathan was supposed to fetch Lester and together they were to relieve him for the evening. He decided that when they got here, he was going to put on his law-and-order face and put an end to this vigil before it became unruly. After all, the multitude had spent the better part of the day venting their anger and paying tribute to Slim. It was time for them to go home. Since the start of this incident, everything about this sorry business grew progressively worse. It would reach an absolute low if the town took the law into their hands. The crowd must disband. Willy needed a break.

The pleasant aroma of fresh coffee drifted in the air. It was a welcome distraction. He got up, lumbered to the potbelly stove, and poured himself another steaming cup.

Before he returned to his chair, he checked on the prisoner in the back room. As he approached the jail cell, the pungent smell of body odor, old spilled whiskey, and stale tobacco replaced the fragrance of coffee. Willy stared through the cold, iron bars in the flicker of the oil lamps. Despite the noise of the protests, Jameson snoozed soundly. He snored like a locomotive struggling to haul its freight up a steep mountain. Funny, but also troubling, that a man who would surely hang in the next few weeks slept as though he hadn't a care in the world. The clamor from the irate citizens of Iron Horse Junction anxious for the chance to tear him to pieces should have induced nervous insomnia in the steeliest individual.

When Jameson was first arrested, Willy figured he was so pickled that his only instinct was to sleep it off. But since Jameson had sobered up, there was no trace of remorse or concern for his fate. The prisoner spent most of his time lying on his cot with his hands behind his head staring dreamily at the blue sky beyond the small, barred window in his cell. Any dialogue with Jameson was short, indifferent, and matter-of-fact. Never did his voice betray a sense of guilt or foreboding of a certain execution. Would a brute like Jameson ever realize the magnitude of the crime he had committed? Didn't he care about the dead man's family? Didn't he have a conscience that told him right from wrong? Probably not. That's why he did what he did and was destined to hang.

Willy settled back into his chair. Jameson's indifference nagged at him almost as much as the shock of Slim's murder. It had to be the cold-hearted nature of the man Willy would never understand. Maybe Jameson didn't fully comprehend or even care that he was going to die miserably for his misdeed.

He heaved another long sigh as he contemplated the awful series of events since he had burst into the Arroyo Saloon seconds after Slim was shot dead by Jameson. There was the swift arrest of Jameson and his two pals, a gut-wrenching notification to Slim's widow, the death notice of the cattle buyer telegraphed to Omaha, the quick swearing in of Nathan and Lester out of necessity to uphold the law in a town buzzing with unlawful retribution, the planning of Slim's funeral, the shipping of the heavily embalmed cattle buyer's corpse to his kin in Omaha, the release of Jameson's pals for lack of evidence over the protests of almost everyone, the somber spectacle of the funeral services, the finality of the burial, and now the nerve-wracking wait for the territorial marshal to arrive and escort the prisoner to Santa Fe for trial.

Adding to his bubbling cauldron of distress was the guilt he felt for not being able to openly express his anguish like most of the townspeople. Slim was his best friend, yet Willy's restrained nature prevented him from crying. The last time he remembered crying, he was six years old and witnessed his dog, Grover, accidentally run over by a buckboard.

He shook his head clear of any further deliberation and resigned himself to the fact that he was overwrought with the burden of the depressing events of the past few days. They were clouding his vision, and it was time to sweep them from his mind. The din outside increased, followed by a hard knocking at the door.

"Uncle Willy, let us in. It's Nathan and Lester."

"Hurrah!" he exclaimed as he sprang from his chair, unbarred the door, and opened it. Nathan and Lester hurried inside while Willy surveyed the crowd from the doorway. The multitude was bigger than he imagined. Almost everyone he knew age ten and older was in the crowd. They, at first, hushed when they saw him, but then began to yell over each other, expressing their anger and the strong desire for grassroots justice.

"All right, everyone, simmer down. I want your attention!" Willy demanded.

The throng pressed forward. Willy slammed the door shut behind him and took a couple of steps toward them. He waved his arms and shouted to be heard. The restive townspeople pushed Willy back, almost pinning him to the door. He managed to pull out his gun and raise it above his head. He fired into the early evening sky. The loud boom produced the intended effect. The crowd became quiet and those nearest to Willy retreated, giving him some breathing room. Most importantly, they riveted their attention to him.

He placed his gun back in his holster and opened his arms, palms up. "Friends, I know you're just as mad as I am. You all know that Slim was more than just my deputy. He was my best friend. I want Jameson hung more than any of you, but as you all know it has to be done by the letter of the law."

"The only letter of the law we're interested is 'H' for hanging," retorted someone in the crowd. "And that's an immediate hanging, so don't forget to add the letter 'I' to your legal alphabet." Uniformly, voices roared approval.

"Looky here, Sheriff, we don't need a spelling lesson in justice," Ted Neely shouted. "He killed Slim and that cattle buyer from Omaha in cold blood. We, the citizens of Iron Horse Junction, demand the right to string up this here polecat. He's gonna hang anyway. Why not by us?" Once again, the crowd resounded their affirmation.

"Yeah," screamed another. "That ought to scare off anyone else who comes to our town and wants to make a nuisance of themselves."

The ruckus rose to a deafening pitch. Many had whipped themselves into a frenzy of scarlet faces and malicious eyes. Now, Willy became truly afraid.

While he considered his next move, the mob's uproar subsided as the Reverend Howard McCallister fought his way through the crowd and stood next to Willy. The Reverend motioned downward with his hands until all protests ceased.

"My brothers and sisters, stop this violent wickedness before it's too late!" ordered the Reverend at the top of his pulpit voice.

All eyes focused on the short, clean-shaven pastor of the town's only church. Clouds had rolled in, but a shaft of the day's waning sunlight pierced through the overcast sky to illuminate the throng. A breeze rustled a few hats and ribbons and caught the reverend's broad-brimmed pilgrim's hat, causing him to place a hand on the crown to hold it firm.

He surveyed the townspeople while building up for the oratorical reprimand that would follow.

"Can't you see that by taking the law into your own hands you are falling into the grip of the devil?" His squinted eyes penetrated the depths of even the nonbelievers. He raised his arms and looked up into the heavens. "Oh, Lord of life, cast out Satan's spell from the souls of your people. Send them back to the virtuous ways taught to us by the most holy Savior."

He put his hands down by his side and stared at the crowd, the stillness broken only by a dog barking in the distance.

Raising his right hand, the preacher, in full fury, pointed at what was now his captivated congregation, "Don't turn our Christian enclave into Sodom and Gomorrah by giving in to riotous revenge. Everyone knows what awaits this imprisoned slaughterer: an agonized departure from the righteous into the gates of hell. It is in the Almighty's design to punish the wicked through divinely inspired laws. Yes, our divinely inspired laws. Have you forgotten that our just rulings originate from a hallowed government whose legislators proudly proclaim, 'in God we trust'?"

Some of the women wiped their eyes. A few of the men murmured contrition.

"I assure you that anyone who partakes in this sinful unruliness will follow this murderer into perdition. Now return to your homes and pray for forgiveness, pray for Slim and his family, for the safety of our town, for your blessings, and for this wretched sinner's soul."

The townspeople dispersed. They shuffled away quietly into the dusk. Reverend McCallister smiled at his triumph. He had saved the wayward citizens of Iron Horse Junction from committing an abomination. It also gave him satisfaction that he wielded such a powerful influence on the citizenry.

"Thank you kindly, Reverend," Willy begrudgingly said.

"Don't thank me. Thank the power of God's grace within me that persuaded these honest citizens to turn away from sin," the reverend replied.

"Well, I can't deny it. It does help to have divine inspiration. Once again, my thanks. Good evening to you, Reverend." Willy tipped his hat and walked toward the doorway.

"You know I haven't seen you and your wife at services in quite a spell."

"We've been busy of late. We'll make a point to get back on the wagon." Willy responded without looking back at the reverend.

"I do hope you'll join us this Sunday. With all the evil that has befallen our Christian community, we'll need everyone's voice in calling on the Lord's mercy to free us from further ruin. Good evening, Sheriff."

"Mmmpf," Willy responded as he opened the heavily reinforced wooden door to his office, still showing his back to the reverend.

Only when he had closed and barred the door did he mutter "Showboater."

Then he looked at Nathan and Lester. They were two of the most opposite looking characters forming a pair. His young, clean-cut nephew, Nathan, and the shifty, one-eyed, bedraggled Lester.

Nathan was a good-looking boy of nineteen. Shy and homespun, he idolized his Uncle Willy. Nathan's mom was Willy's beloved sister, and Willy cherished her boy almost as much as she did. The bond between Willy and Nathan grew even stronger after Nathan lost his father in a railroad accident. Willy and his wife, Lucy, were childless, which further strengthened the relationship between uncle and nephew. He watched the boy grow into manhood with the love and pride he would have bestowed on his own son.

The tall, lean Nathan wanted to be like his Uncle Willy in every way, including the aspiration to become a law officer. Willy was unsure that a good-natured boy like Nathan was suited for the rough side of upholding the law. After months of Nathan's pleading, Willy relented when his sister finally gave her tacit approval. When Slim's unfortunate murder created the vacancy, Willy deputized Nathan.

Lester was another story. Willy wanted a second deputy to serve part time as needed. The town's one-eyed handyman was eager to oblige. A black patch covered his right eye, lost in a stick fight when he was a child. He lived in a ramshackle hut just outside of town. He had no actual trade, so he supported his wife and eight kids by scrounging up any of the town's odd jobs. The balding, disheveled man looked forward to another source of income. His impoverished family rejoiced in his good fortune.

"You boys better stay on your toes all night. Those townspeople may have a change of heart once they get home. Speaking of home, that's where I'm going. I need a hot meal and a warm bed. You're not allowed to let anyone in, do you hear?"

"Don't worry, Uncle Willy. We won't let anyone in. We promise," Nathan replied.

"If there's any more trouble, one of you needs to come get me. The other needs to stay put, guarding the prisoner. If either of you can't leave the jail, unshutter one of the windows and fire a couple of shots into the air. I'll come a runnin'. Understand?"

"We hear ya loud and clear, Sheriff," Lester answered in his slow drawl.

"Okay, I'll check the prisoner and head home. Remember to check on him every fifteen minutes and leave your guns on the desk. We don't want Jameson reaching through the bars and grabbing someone's pistol."

"Yeah, good idea, Uncle Willy. Don't worry we'll take care of everything. You go home and get yourself some well-deserved rest. We'll see you in the morning. Be sure to say 'hi' to Aunt Lucy for me," Nathan replied.

Warily, Willy looked at them but convinced himself that the horrendous chain of events had entered a lull. They should be all right as long as they stayed barricaded within the jail.

"And make sure you keep the windows shuttered and bar the door when I leave. Just stay vigilant and, for heaven's sake, don't either of you doze off. There's plenty of coffee and a deck of cards to keep you awake."

He looked at them for one last time, shook his head, checked on Jameson, and left the two greenhorn deputies. With each step toward home, he had to fight off the growing urge to return to the jail. Jameson's calm manner still troubled Willy. It was an oddity that raised storm-warning flags in his mind, even though there were no dark clouds on the horizon. Something wasn't right.

But another voice in his head overtook the urge. It told him he was overreacting to the adversity surrounding him. He had to get a hold on himself and think clearly. Everything was under control, and there was no need to manufacture any more mischief. With that, he moseyed home to his hot meal, a warm bed, and affectionate wife.

# *Chapter 6*

The town of Millbrook faded into the distance. More than once, Ben glanced back not in regret but in uncertainty. Would this be the last time he would see Rachel? She wanted to marry him, and on one occasion he had promised that he would marry her. It was a rash statement made during a tender moment after lovemaking. How could he have said that? He was still reeling from the bitter marital experience with Nora prior to her death. His long absences as a roving marshal had taken their toll on their marriage. Out of loneliness and spite, she sought the company of other men. When he discovered her infidelities, he started to drink heavily and had trysts of his own. The last few years of their marriage, he avoided her completely. They communicated only when necessary via the post or telegraph.

Compounding his miserable marital experience was the awkward circumstance of falling in love with Rachel, Nora's sister. After Nora's funeral, their relationship started out as an innocent gesture of mutual consolation. Somehow, it blossomed into a love affair. It was a predicament that made the ultimate union between them uncomfortable for him. No matter how many times Rachel tried to convince him that there was nothing wrong, he couldn't come to grips with the fact that he'd be wed to his departed wife's sister.

When Millbrook finally disappeared over a knoll, he reminisced about how it got started.

> *A fellow marshal sought him out at a bordello in Santa Fe and gave him the urgent telegram announcing Nora's death due to typhoid. Through red, bleary eyes from a night of heavy drinking and sex, he struggled to grasp the impact of the news. With the help of the compassionate marshal, he stumbled back to his hotel room. His pathetic condition caught the attention of the innkeeper, who had known Ben for many years as a likeable, repeat customer. He helped take Ben up the stairs and came to find out the cause leading to Ben's wretched state.*
>
> *Eventually, reality sunk in. Ben's muddled mind's reaction was to find solace in more whiskey. He would have drunk himself to death if it wasn't for the intervention of the concerned innkeeper, who came to check on him.*
>
> *Ben didn't respond to the continuous knocking and pleas from the innkeeper. A Mexican priest, Father Bonaventura, with a novice from the cathedral, had been visiting an old friend in a room down the hall. Distracted by the commotion, the short, round, jovial priest and a few hotel guests in other rooms had*

28

*filed into the hallway. When the innkeeper was forced to open the door using a passkey, the priest and the novice followed him into the room. That's where they found Ben unconscious, lying face down on the bed. Empty bottles of whiskey were strewn about the room.*

*They dragged him out to the vacant lot behind the hotel. While Father Bonaventura and the innkeeper held him up on his knees, the novice fetched an emetic from a pharmacist, who was awoken to deal with the emergency. The priest forced Ben to drink from a small vial of bitter herbs. He vomited everything out of his gut. In between the cramps and urges to vomit further, they forced him to drink lots of water. When he appeared to be relieved of most of his distress, they helped him up to his room.*

*Father Bonaventura and the novice watched over him for the remainder of the night. The next day they switched him to black coffee. The priest sent the novice back to the cathedral and proceeded to commiserate with Ben. For Ben, this was one of the most important moments of his life. He had never been a religious man. His parents never belonged to any organized church. They were decent people, but they were never churchgoers. Consequently, Ben grew up with good principles and only a sense that there was a God somewhere out there.*

*Father Bonaventura made a lasting impression on him. Not that Ben became spiritual. Instead, it sobered him up from that day forward. He retook positive control of his life and swore off liquor. It was the second time a stranger came to his rescue during a life-threatening crisis. The first time, two burly young men saved him from being beaten to death by a crowd of drunken miners. The miners were upset when an exceptionally pretty bar girl abruptly left their company to join Ben when he entered the saloon. Outraged, they dragged the youthful Ben, who had just arrived in Santa Fe to apply for an open position as a territorial marshal, into the street in front of the saloon, where they took turns pounding him. Just as Ben was about to lose consciousness, these two strapping youths came from nowhere and joined the fray. They fought the miners to a standstill until all of them scattered just ahead of the arrival of the town's law officers. Before they fled, one of his defenders gently turned Ben on his back and tapped him on the cheek to see if he was alive. Ben would never forget the happy look on*

*the young man's rough-hewn face when he opened his eyes.*
*Before he could utter "thank you" from his broken body, the*
*young man took off.*

*Now there was Father Bonaventura. How the priest touched*
*him was the closest thing to his idea of a miracle. The good-*
*hearted cleric consoled Ben and gave him words of*
*encouragement. He spoke of forgiveness and of enduring the*
*world's suffering as the man Jesus had done hundreds of years*
*before. Father Bonaventura never tried to convert Ben but*
*made a point to let him know that everyone has a purpose in*
*this world and needed to do his best to make the most of it.*
*Before the kindly priest left, he bestowed a blessing upon Ben*
*in a language Ben had never heard. The priest ended the*
*blessing by moving his right hand vertically and then*
*horizontally. His parting words were something Ben would*
*often contemplate, "Remember, wherever you go, God goes*
*with you."*

Eventually, distracted by the vast emptiness of the landscape and the growing distance from Millbrook, Ben's apprehension eased. Not that it disappeared completely, but at least it was waning as his thoughts shifted more toward the transfer of the murderer from Iron Horse Junction to Santa Fe.

The horse, rider, and pack mule picked their way through the sunbaked country of scrub and parched earth. The animals' plodding hooves kicked up puffs of dust. Their flanks were starting to lather, and he knew he must stop soon to give them water. The sun at close to midday heated the landscape, causing most creatures to lie listless in shaded areas until the relief of sunset. Ben's caravan, a lone wandering coyote, and the occasional whirling dust devil were the only disturbances in the motionless hot terrain.

At last, the small party came to what appeared to be a dried-out streambed. Luckily, a rivulet of water was winding its way through the stony bed. The horse and mule made a beeline for the trickling water and lapped it up as if their thirst was unquenchable. Ben went upstream and refilled his canteens. It was late afternoon. They had gone about twenty-five miles, and he was pleased with their progress. A few more miles and he would reach the old abandoned Spanish mission of San Miguel. It was a group of rundown church buildings that he and other wayfarers availed themselves of when necessary. It had a well, and, although the buildings were roofless, he could find shelter in one of the former friars' quarters in what was the main building. Tomorrow, he hoped to make it to Fort Bascomb by nightfall. If not, he was prepared to sleep under the stars, although he preferred to spend the night indoors.

By dusk they reached the old mission. As they clomped toward the open plaza amidst the rundown structures, Ben found the place deserted. Remains from recent campfires littered the landscape. He halted at the entrance to the main building that had housed the monks. Remnants of rotted wood hung on rusty hinges that once held large, impressive double doors leading into the heart of the monastery. Tying his horse and the mule to a worn hitching post, he made his way to the larger abbot's quarters. They were empty and, most importantly, uncluttered by previous visitors. Within a few minutes, Ben unsaddled his horse and brought in all his belongings. As he had so many times before, he made himself a comfortable encampment in the room's roofless confines. The horse and mule he brought into the monks' quarters next door, using the same old wooden gate he had found on a previous trip to keep them penned in. He took the saddle off of his horse and the pack of off the mule and removed both animals' reins. There were two wooden buckets sitting in the corner. These he had scrounged on a previous trip and took delight that they were still there. He took the buckets to the well, filled them, and watered Betsy, his black-spotted saddle horse, and the mule. In one of the large pockets of one of the packs was a blanket of pressed hay. He tore off two large chunks and fed his beasts of burden. Before leaving, he rubbed both their snouts in affection and appreciation.

Just outside the entrance, he built a fire from wood scraps he found scattered throughout the grounds and began cooking his dinner. The strong smell of bacon, beans, and coffee hung around the campfire. Twilight became night, and the crackling flames flickered against the sunbaked adobe walls that surrounded the open plaza.

Ben thought he heard something and looked up and around. It sounded like a light rush of wind. He didn't see anyone. He turned over the bacon and looked up again. A group of more than a dozen Indians dressed in traditional Jicarilla Apache garb stood directly in front of the campfire. They were grim-faced. Some wore feathers, and others had bandanas. Some wore faded shirts, and others were naked above the waist, with beads around their necks that dropped down their chests. All wore britches and moccasins. None wore war paint.

Motionless, they stared at him. A few held rifles close to their chests. The firelight flickered on their torsos. Careful not to show fear, Ben slowly stood up and made sure his empty hands were within plain view. On the other side of the campfire he recognized an old friend who wore an unbuttoned blue coat over his naked chest.

Ben raised his open right hand to shoulder level in greeting. "Blue Jacket, welcome, my friend. It has been a long time since we've enjoyed each other's company."

The tall, swarthy man that Ben recognized smiled and reciprocally raised his right hand in greeting. The well-traveled blue coat the Indian wore had been stripped from a dead U.S. dragoon by his father at the Battle of Cieneguilla. Blue Jacket was a big man with jet-black eyes and long, raven hair held in place by a red headband. A large beaded necklace hung close to his neck.

"Marshal Ben, it has been many sunrises since we last met."

"Why are you and your braves traveling a great distance from your reservation?"

Blue Jacket dropped his right hand, and his smile disappeared. "There is much sorrow among my people. We have lost our tribal lands. Your great chief breaks our treaties. We have no future, only the past. We are on our way to make ceremony at the sacred place of our ancestors on the Rio Moro to ask them for their help."

Although Ben was outnumbered, duty compelled him to make a statement. "Blue Jacket, you know that you're in violation of the treaty by coming out here. If word gets out that you are roaming your old tribal lands, the horse soldiers will hunt you down. There will be more bloodshed, and your people will suffer more harm."

"We do not want trouble with the white man or his horse soldiers, but we have no choice. We must go to the sacred ground and beg our ancestors' spirits to save our people or we will be no more."

Ben had experience with Blue Jacket and his band of braves before. Twice he had had to lead them back to their reservation and warn them not to venture into the countryside without consulting the Indian agent. This had to be another Jicarilla raiding party intending to grab what they could of value from the white man's realm. The explanation given by Blue Jacket was a pretext. It's true that they weren't looking for a direct confrontation with the horse soldiers or anyone else. They were looking to steal by stealth, and they had to do it quickly before they were discovered missing by the Indian agent at the Tierra Amarilla reservation.

He also sympathized with the plight of the Jicarilla Apaches. The white man's encroachment and constant war with the Comanche had devastated them. They tried to fight back in the Battle of Cieneguilla in 1854. It was a brief victory followed by utter defeat at the hands of the U.S. cavalry. Since then, there had been many treaties made and broken by the U.S. government. This forced them to move to several places, depending on the treaty, before finally settling at Tierra Amarilla. White man's diseases and too much firewater added to their misery.

As a result, the Jicarilla resorted to stealing what they could not otherwise obtain to support themselves: horses, cattle, guns, ammunition, clothing, even food stocks. Raiding parties like the one led by Blue Jacket were common. Since their forays produced no injury or loss of life, the Jicarilla knew that if caught the extent of their punishment would be to give up their stolen goods and return to the reservation. As a marshal of New Mexico Territory, Ben had an obligation to uphold the law and force the Jicarilla to restore anything they stole before leading them back to Tierra Amarilla. He had to deal with them tactfully in order to avoid another full-scale Indian uprising.

"How many days have you been gone from the reservation?"

"Many days. It takes much time to move through our old tribal lands because we must avoid the white man's villages and farms." Blue Jacket paused and stared intently into Ben's eyes.

"Have you taken anything that does not belong to you? If you have, you must return it immediately before you go back to Tierra Amarilla." He nervously waited for Blue Jacket's response.

"We have hunted and taken only what we need to eat, nothing else."

"And the white man…are you sure that you made no contact with the white man?"

Blue Jacket knew that Ben was anxious to find out whether he and his braves had even the slightest interaction with the white settlers, even eye contact. "We have avoided all along our way. We travel as hidden as our ancestors' spirits."

Ben took a half-sigh of relief. Hopefully, Blue Jacket told the truth. Then the worst that could happen was either the band of Indians would be sighted and reported or they would finally be discovered missing at Tierra Amarilla.

"We have had this talk many times. You must never leave the reservation. It leads to trouble. I can't take you back because I have another duty that I must perform. But you must go back now and not take anything that does not belong to you."

With resolve Blue Jacket replied, "Ben, I know you as a friend. That is why I have shown my braves and myself. I trust you would understand the happiness of my people rests on prayers at the sacred ground." Then he raised his voice and said, "We must go. We will go!"

Ben was startled. Before he could respond, Blue Jacket lowered his voice and, in a friendlier manner, added, "We will return to Tierra Amarilla after our ceremony on the holy ground. I speak the truth."

Ben grimaced as he strained to think of an appropriate yet firm way to order them back. They had to return to the reservation immediately. But....

He rubbed the nape of his neck, allowing Blue Jacket's unyielding stance to settle in. Blue Jacket and his party were on a mission that no one could deter. Even if it meant that they would have to fight to the last man. Further demands that the Indians return to the reservation weren't going to work.

"I do not approve of your journey, but I do understand. I want to remain your trusted friend. I wish I didn't have this duty that I must perform. I would go with you to the River Moro and then lead you back to Tierra Amarilla. Go then in peace, avoiding the white man as you have done, not taking anything that does not belong to you, and return directly to the reservation. Tomorrow I will be in Fort Bascomb. I will tell them that you and your men are on a peaceful mission to the holy grounds on the River Moro. I cannot say what the cavalry will do, so do not stay long. I will do my best to assure them that you mean no harm and that you will return immediately to the reservation."

"Thank you, Ben. You have always been a good friend to our people. Now let us sit by the fire and talk of many things as friends. In white-man's fashion, Blue Jacket extended his hand to Ben, who immediately grabbed hold of it and shook it.

Blue Jacket's braves relaxed, laughing and sighing in relief. The men with rifles dropped them to their sides, and a couple of them came up to Ben to shake his hand in white-man's fashion.

For the rest of the evening, they cooked, ate, and spoke in a festive atmosphere. The only thing of which Ben did not partake was the bottle of whiskey that Blue Jacket and his braves passed around.

In the camaraderie of the evening, the Jicarilla demonstrated why Ben liked them. Despite their reputation as brutal savages, they had proven to him many times that they were decent people brought up in a different way of life. He valued their friendship because they, in turn, held him in respect—a respect he earned with his fair treatment, even though many times they disagreed. He hoped someday that they and the white man would bury the hatchet and resolve their differences through acceptance and cooperation. Realistically, he never thought he would live to see it happen.

The next day Ben and the party of Jicarilla Apaches said goodbye. The Indians resumed their journey to the River Moro. Ben headed out into the rugged terrain in the direction of Fort Bascomb. He really didn't know how the commanding officer at Fort Bascomb would react to a band of Indians roaming the countryside. Ben was betting that after he explained the reason for the Indian's excursion, the worst thing that would happen was that a patrol would be sent out to make sure that the Indians returned quickly and peacefully to Tierra Amarilla after their pilgrimage. Nobody wanted to risk another Indian war. At least, that's what he told himself over and over.

# *Chapter 7*

In Iron Horse Junction, just before the faint glow of daybreak, two men crept toward the secured door of the sheriff's office. The whole frontage of the sheriff's office was enveloped in the cover of night. The once-flickering lanterns on both sides of the door had long run out of oil. A new moon and the town's lack of street lamps aided the men's concealment.

One man cradled a small barrel filled with gunpowder. Its heavy weight caused him to grimace. He strained to hold it against his chest while creeping toward the door, stifling his labored breathing as best as he could. The only other sound was the slight jingle of his spurs. These he couldn't afford to discard since they were needed to prod his horse for a fast getaway after the deed.

The other man followed directly behind him with his gun drawn. His eyes scanned the dark, deserted street for the town's early risers. Since it was Sunday morning, the chance of any routine pre-dawn activity would be slim. He wasn't breathing as heavily as his partner but provided an accompanying light clinking from his spurs.

Despite Sheriff Gibson's strict orders, Nathan and Lester had fallen asleep. Lester was the first to go. Sometime after midnight, he decided that nothing was really going to happen. He chose repose over vigilance. Putting two chairs in front of the sheriff's desk, he made himself comfortable and dozed off while Nathan chattered some nonsense about upholding their sworn duty.

Nathan tried his best to stay awake. Several cups of coffee made him jittery but could not suppress the early-to-bed regimen he had lived his whole life. Without Lester's wakeful company, he succumbed to slumber sitting upright in the chair behind Willy's desk with his arms folded.

In the back room, Jameson had his hat, kerchief, and boots on. He stood by his cell door staring in the direction of the dozing deputies. The door between the sheriff's office and the back room was open, but from his vantage he could only hear them snoring. His view was limited to the dimly lit, bare office space that led to a shuttered front window. On the day after his arrest, his two friends had tossed him a note through the small barred window to his cell, promising to bust him out of jail. This morning they tossed him another note saying the jail break would occur just before dawn. The note went on to advise him to move his bunk to the farthest corner of his cell away from the front of the sheriff's office and to get behind it and wait. But Jameson was anxious and couldn't resist getting a front row seat to whatever action his pals were going to unleash to free him.

Outside, the husky man carrying the barrel placed it next to the door. He pulled a cork plug from the top of the barrel and stuffed a short fuse into the opening, anchoring it in the gunpowder. After wiping his sweaty brow with his sleeve, he pulled a match from his vest pocket and looked back at his partner. The other taller man tapped him on the shoulder in approval. The match was struck, and the fuse lit. While it hissed and sparked, the men ran to the side of the building and dropped to the ground.

The fizzling sound woke Nathan with a start. He jumped to his feet.

"Lester, do you hear that? For heaven's sake will you wake...."

A bright flash penetrated the tiny, open space between the front door and the floor. It was followed by a thunderous explosion, which blew the door to pieces, disintegrated a large section of the wall around the door, and dropped the ceiling toward the opening created by the blast.

Nathan was hurled against the wall behind the desk. His stunned body dropped off the wall, and he hit the floor headfirst. Dazed and hurting all over, he struggled to get up on all fours, coughing violently in the stifling cloud of dust that filled the room. The ringing in his head was so loud he thought his skull was going to burst. He felt blood dripping out of both ears, his nose, and his mouth. All the oil lamps had gone out, but there was a growing light from a fire created by spilt oil from one of the lamps at the other end of the room.

The two men responsible for the explosion burst into the room through the gaping hole where the door used to be, brandishing their pistols. Their kerchiefs were pulled over their mouths as they searched the dust-choked room in the glow of the small fire. They had trouble seeing through the haze, but they heard Nathan's coughing fit and moved towards him. As Nathan tried to look in their direction, they pumped several rounds into him. Nathan gave a cry and crumpled to the floor.

"Go find them keys," the taller of the two men ordered. "I'll take care of the other one and check on Frank. Hurry!"

Lester's body had been thrown in front of the doorway leading to the back room. He was lying motionless in the fetal position. The taller man aimed his pistol at Lester's head and pulled the trigger twice, blowing away the back of Lester's skull in splashes of blood, bone, and brain matter. He grabbed Lester by the back of his jacket and hauled his limp body away from the doorway.

"Damn! Where the hell are them keys?" shouted the shorter, stouter man as he desperately rummaged around what was left of the desk. "I can barely see anything. Where'd they put them?"

"Look in them drawers. They usually keep them in there. Hurry!" the taller man replied before heading to the back room. "Frank, are you there? It's me, Callahan. Are you okay?"

"Yeah, considering I survived a direct hit from a canon," Jameson replied dusting himself off and coughing a couple of times.

There was light from a single oil lamp farthest from the door. The glass bulb had been knocked off, but the lamp weakly illuminated the murky back room. The concussion from the explosion had littered the area with all kinds of debris.

"Well, I warned you to take cover. It ain't my fault if you don't listen."

"Never mind. We gotta get out of here. That blast was loud enough to wake the whole territory. Them townspeople is itchin' to string me up something fierce. They'll be here in short order. Open this here cell."

"Bledsoe's looking for the keys," Callahan stated matter-of-factly.

"Forget the keys," an exasperated Jameson countered. "Just put your gun barrel into the keyhole and shoot until the lock breaks."

Callahan complied. Unfortunately, when he pulled the trigger, all he got was a click from his spent pistol. "Dang it," he exclaimed.

"I found them," an exuberant Bill Bledsoe shouted as he ran into the back room holding the ring of keys triumphantly above his head. "They were right in one of them drawers just like you said, Callahan. Hey, Frank, ready to be sprung?"

"Would ya' get me the hell outta here!" Jameson yelled in frustration.

Bledsoe quickly worked down the ring. Callahan had just finished reloading his revolver when the third key on the ring opened the cell door.

Jameson burst out of the cell. "Move, before we end up the main attraction at a triple hangin' in this goddamn place!"

They rushed through the sheriff's office, where the fire was now raging through half of the room opposite the corpses and the shattered desk. Billows of gray smoke mixed with the thick airborne dust. Jameson gagged and raised his kerchief to cover his mouth. As they charged toward the demolished entrance, flames licked their arms.

When they were clear of the building, Jameson lowered his kerchief, spat out the horrible taste in his mouth, and with watery eyes asked, "Which way?"

Bledsoe and Callahan rubbed their stinging eyes, lowered their kerchiefs, and pointed down the street. With hacking coughs, they took off in that direction. On the way, they raced past a few startled townspeople who had rushed outside. Some called out to the running trio, asking what happened. The three miscreants ignored them. They made it to a side street where three horses were tied to a hitching rail. Bledsoe pointed Jameson to his horse.

Without further incident, they quickly untied the horses and safely galloped out of town.

*　　*　　*

The blast shocked Willy and Lucy into awakened terror. The house shuddered. The bed shook. The sound of breaking glass was everywhere. Dust flew from fresh cracks in the walls. Lucy screamed. Willy shot to a sitting position only to be conked on the head by a large chunk of dislodged plaster from the ceiling. He was out cold.

When he regained consciousness, he was lying on the floor and Lucy was wiping the swollen wound on his forehead with a wet towel. He didn't know where he was or what had happened. The right side of his forehead near the hairline throbbed.

"Lucy?"

"Willy, the jail blew up. It's on fire," she wailed. "Lord have mercy. Nathan's in there."

"What?" he roared.

Willy jumped up, disregarding the aching head wound. He stumbled to the curtained window facing the street. What greeted him when he opened the curtains was like something out of the depths of Dante's *Inferno*. Through a newly cracked window, he witnessed the surreal sight of the sheriff's office consumed in flames. The conflagration shot up two or three stories. In the feeble daylight, people half in their sleeping attire and half in their regular clothes made up bucket brigades trying to douse the fire.

A rapid, hard knocking on his front door interrupted his gaze. Lucy went and opened the door.

"Mrs. Gibson, where's the sheriff?" an excited Ted Neely asked while removing his hat. "Doesn't he know that the jail is burning to the ground?" He, too, was half-dressed in his light gray sleeping shirt but had his distinctive black bowler in his hand and wore his black trousers and black boots.

"I'm here, Ted," a squinting-in-pain Willy replied as he appeared at the door in his faded red long johns. He was pressing the palm of his hand on his head injury. As he proceeded to explain, he dropped the hand to his side. "I got knocked out when a piece of the ceiling hit me on the head."

Even in the dull light of daybreak, Willy's head wound was noticeable.

"My, you got crowned. Are you all right? Do you want me to fetch the doctor?"

"Yes, please fetch Doc Finster," Lucy answered. "I'll put Willy to bed after I clean the mess made by the ceiling."

"No, that won't be necessary. I'm all right, I tell you," Willy protested as he resumed rubbing the contusion. He looked at Lucy and gently said, "I'm the sheriff. I gotta go take charge." Then he turned to Ted and asked, "Did Nathan or Lester explain what happened?"

There was a long pause. Willy ignored the nagging bump on the head and focused on Ted Neely's grim face.

"Now, sheriff, I hate to always be the bearer of bad news...."

"Ted!" Willy shouted. "Where's my nephew? ... Lester? ... Jameson? What happened?"

"It's a jail break," Ted exclaimed. "Jameson's two pals blew out the front door and broke him out of jail. A few of the townspeople saw them ride the hell out of town. It was still dark, but they passed close enough to a bartender, the blacksmith, and some others who swear it was them."

For almost a minute, an unbearable, highly charged silence followed. No one wanted to ask the next obvious question.

"We haven't found Nathan or Lester," Ted blurted. "As far as we know, they haven't come out of the building. It's possible they were caught up in a gun fight. People heard several shots shortly after the explosion."

"Oh, my Lord!" Lucy shrieked.

Willy shook his head and grabbed Lucy's hand, "Now, Lucy, don't jump to conclusions." Then he turned to Ted. "Hold it. Maybe my nephew and Lester, after the gun battle, were tied and gagged or just plain knocked out."

"Sheriff," Ted said sternly, "the whole building is on fire. If anyone's in there, it's not likely they'll come out...alive. At this point, no one mortal can go in there to look for them with the heat, smoke, fire, and all."

Lucy dropped to her knees, sobbing.

"Well, maybe they're not in there," Willy replied, releasing Lucy's hand. Shaking both hands palms up at Ted, he countered. "Maybe they fled from the building during the gun fight."

"Then why haven't they showed themselves?" Ted refuted.

Willy's eyes widened, and his face froze. Except for the red knot on his forehead, his skin turned white. The sound and motion of his breathing was imperceptible.

"Sheriff, are you okay?" Ted asked nervously. "I'm sorry to have to be the one to tell you this. I'm...awful...sorry." Ted shifted his attention to Lucy, whose sobbing became louder. "Mrs. Gibson, I'm truly sorry."

Running out of words, Ted uttered, "If only you would've let us string up Jameson. Then his gang would have no cause to...."

"Aaaahhh!!!" screamed Willy. It was so shrill that Ted recoiled in surprise.

Willy knelt next to his wife. He put his arms around her, and she put her arms around him. Together they wept.

Ted Neely turned and left them without saying goodbye. As the town's undertaker, he knew how to console grieving people who had lost a loved one. This was a rare occasion when he didn't know what to do.

\*    \*    \*

Within three hours, the townspeople had the blaze under control. Every inch of the building was charred. Parts of it were burned to the ground. The bars of the jail were the only things that appeared untouched. They stood as a monument of defiance to the catastrophe that surrounded them.

It took at least another couple of hours for the heat to subside so that a search party could enter the smoldering ruin. Predictably, they found the badly burned remains of Nathan and Lester. Ted Neely, serving as coroner, identified the gunshot wounds to both, indicating that they had been spared the agonizing torment of burning to death. It brought little consolation to Willy and Lucy Gibson, Nathan's widowed mother, or Lester's impoverished widow and his eight fatherless children.

# Chapter 8

The lone rider with a pack mule in tow approached the large, wooden gates of Fort Bascomb a couple of hours after sunset. He could have easily lost his way if it weren't for the distant glow of lighted torches within the fort that served as his beacon. Their radiance rose into the black, moonless sky, spurring him on as the light became brighter with every step his horse took.

He stopped in front of the gates. The trickle of light that escaped over the high rounded adobe wall cast enough illumination to announce his arrival. He looked up at the silhouettes of two soldiers on guard duty perched behind a waist-high wall above the gates. Behind them, amber light from blazing torches flickered. They pointed their rifles at him.

"Ho there," he shouted.

"Ho there, yourself," one of them challenged. "Who are you and what do you want?"

"I'm a New Mexico marshal looking for a night's shelter."

"That so," said the other one.

The two soldiers spoke to one another in hushed tones. Another soldier appeared, briefly joined their discussion, and called out with an Irish brogue. "What's your name, fella? And why, by all the saints in heaven, are you roaming this Godforsaken country at night? Are you daft, man?"

"No crazier than you, Sergeant O'Malley, when you left the Emerald Isle to come to this miserable place," Ben replied, delighted that he recognized the good-natured Sergeant.

"Glory be, if it isn't the only teetotaler marshal in this celebrated territory of New Mexico. Don't shoot him, lads, he's a one-of-a-kind wonder."

The soldiers lowered their rifles and laughed.

"Tell me, Marshal Ben Corrigan, how's life without the elixir of whiskey treating you? Or have you come to your senses and realize that the world is an extremely dull place without the pleasures of a libation?"

The other two soldiers laughed louder.

"Well, I'd be happy to talk to you about my conversion to temperance if you wouldn't mind opening the gates for me."

42

"Would you now. Lads, open the gates for this poor wayward creature. Don't you know it's an honor to welcome any law officer that aspires to sainthood through abstinence? Which is to say, this fine lawman won't consume any of our liquor, so why not let him in?"

All three soldiers gave an even hardier laugh.

The heavy wooden doors to the adobe fort swung open. Ben rode into a large open space that served as a staging area and parade ground, lit by blazing torches. A number of crude wooden dwellings occupied the entire perimeter of the square fort. The largest building at the end farthest from the gates was the soldiers' barracks. This was where travelers could find a place to sleep, since there was always extra room.

Just in front of the barracks was the commandant's quarters. An empty flagpole—the American flag was taken down after "Taps"—stood in front of the steps leading to the porch and main entrance to the building.

Sergeant O'Malley met him at the flagpole. As Ben dismounted, the sergeant grabbed the horse's reins with one hand and stroked Betsy's snout with the other.

"Betsy, how's my pretty *cailín?*" the Sergeant said tenderly. Betsy snorted, bobbed her head, pawed the ground, and flicked her tail in mutual affection. "And by the way, a good evening to you, Marshal Ben Corrigan," he said with a smirk, offering his hand to Ben. "I'll wager I know what brings you to Fort Bascomb. Could it be that you're on your way to perform your constabulary duties at the thriving community of Iron Horse Junction?"

Ben shook the hand of the sergeant and eyed him in friendly suspicion. "Howdy, Sergeant. Good to see you again. How did you know I was on my way to Iron Horse Junction?"

"Well, I have to confess. A young marshal companion of yours by the name of Eddie Blake stopped here yesterday on his way to the very same town. He knew from a telegraph you sent from Millbrook to the marshal's office in Santa Fe that you would probably stop at the fort—like you usually do when you're coming through this part of the territory. He knows you well, doesn't he?"

"Yeah, he's new, and I told him all the popular overnight stops between Santa Fe and Texas. Is that all?"

Sergeant O'Malley's voice took a more humorless tone. "He asked me to give you a message, and it's not one I care to tell you."

"And that is?"

"He said to tell you these three things. One, the prisoner escaped with the help of two accomplices. Two, they burned down the jail and killed two deputies—may God have mercy on their departed souls. Finally, get to Iron Horse Junction as quickly as you can. He'll meet you there along with another marshal. I believe his name is George…George Whitmore."

Ben reeled back in disbelief. He searched the sergeant's face to see whether he was in jest. "You wouldn't be making this up or stretching it a bit?"

"Not this time," the sergeant said earnestly. "I couldn't be more serious."

"This is God-awful," Ben exclaimed. "That man who broke out of jail killed a cattle buyer in a saloon and then shot dead the town's deputy. Now this."

"That town is under Satan's spell, to be sure," the sergeant declared.

"Did Marshal Blake mention whether other marshals have been sent to Iron Horse Junction?"

"Nary a word."

"Thanks, Sergeant," Ben said, tactfully avoiding sarcasm. "You've always had a good memory for detail. Why haven't they made you a general by now?"

"In due time, my good man. In due time," the sergeant replied. "It's to my sorrow, it is, that I'm the one that was charged to pass along these bad tidings to yourself. Next time, I'll tell the lad to leave any tales of woe with the commandant."

"Sergeant O'Malley, a marshal's life is never predictable. It's something I've learned to enjoy and other times regret. This particular regret is coming at a bad time." He thought about Rachel and the unpredictable delay that would follow this unexpected turn of events.

"So, goes another day in the life of a champion of justice," the Sergeant declared. But noticing his effort to lighten the mood had fallen short, he returned his attention to stroking Betsy's muzzle.

"This means I'll have to leave at first light to make sure I get there by nightfall. I need to speak to the commandant before I go. It's important. Blue Jacket and a band of Jicarilla Indians have left the reservation. They are on their way to the River Moro."

"Saints alive," replied the sergeant.

"They're not out to cause trouble. They're on a pilgrimage to their holy grounds to pray for their people. I ran into them last night at the old mission of

San Miguel. They won't go back to Tierra Amarillo until they perform their ritual."

"Then you best go to it, lad. You may be able to catch the new commandant before he retires for the night. I'll look after your darling Betsy and that scruffy looking baggage train you call a mule."

"Thanks. And by the way, the mule's name also happens to be O'Malley," Ben replied as he hurried up the steps.

"Ha," retorted the sergeant.

When Ben reached the door the sergeant shouted, "When you're done, I'll meet you at the soldier's mess."

He halted momentarily. Took off his hat. Gave the door a couple of light knocks.
Walked in hoping he could muster a convincing argument concerning the Jicarillas' sojourn to their holy site, despite his new preoccupation with the turn of events in Iron Horse Junction.

*   *   *

Colonel Parker puffed on his cigar as he pondered all that Ben had told him. He leaned against the mantle in his dark-blue flannel robe. His round face, surrounded by a white cloud of smoke, frowned thoughtfully into the empty firebox of the massive stone fireplace. The newly installed commander of Fort Bascomb had just fallen asleep when his aide woke him to tell him that a New Mexico marshal was waiting to talk to him about a band of Jicarilla Apache Indians roaming the countryside.

The four oil lamps, one in each corner, struggled to illuminate the rustic office, in which walls of stacked dark-brown logs absorbed most of the light. A large wooden desk dominated the floor space. Piles of paper covered every inch of the desktop. A bookcase filled with leather-bound legal and territorial books was at one end of the room. The red-white-and-blue regimental colors and some Indian trophies—headdresses, spears, bows, and arrows—were proudly displayed in a corner at the other end. Two worn wooden chairs stood in front of the desk. Ben was next to one of them. He was too nervous to sit.

"I assure you, Colonel, this band of Indians is on a peaceful mission. A patrol of safe conduct is all that is necessary," Ben reiterated as he stood fidgeting with his hat.

The colonel pulled the cigar from his mouth, "I hear you, Marshal. But a band of armed Indians wandering about in violation of their treaty is something I can't take lightly. How do you know they haven't lied to you? They may be pillaging the countryside as we speak. They've done it before," he said, narrowing his eyes.

"I can't say for sure," Ben conceded. "All I can say is that they came across to me as genuine. I can also tell you that they are determined. Any attempt to force them to turn back would probably end up in a pretty nasty fight."

"So, you want me to send a small escort to make sure they stay out of trouble? What happens if they take offense to the patrol and decide to attack?" the colonel shot back. "Then I'll jeopardize the lives of those men more so then sending a larger force in the first place. I don't see any other choice but to send the largest detachment I have and haul them back to their Tierra Amarillo. If they get wiped out in a confrontation, it'll send a message to their red tribesmen to stay put and stay out of trouble."

"Look, Colonel, I'm telling you what I know from experience and what I understand from last night's parley with Blue Jacket. If you don't show some measure of restraint for these people, we'll end up in another Indian war. Seeing that they are desperate, it'll be a pure bloodbath for both sides."

"Just whose side are you on marshal?" the colonel pointedly asked.

Ben clenched his jaw and glowered at the colonel. "I'm a sworn marshal for this territory. My job is to enforce its laws and promote the peace for all who reside in New Mexico. By treating the Indians with some measure of respect, the peace and security of everyone is improved."

Colonel Parker resumed smoking his cigar, staring back at Ben.

"Now I've said my piece. If you'll excuse me, I need to turn in. I have to leave at first light for Iron Horse Junction."

"Certainly, Marshal. I'll think about what you said before I make my decision. Good evening to you."

"Good evening, Colonel."

# Chapter 9

Ben entered the outskirts of Iron Horse Junction around six o'clock in the evening. A couple of ragged dogs roamed the deserted street leading to the town center. The houses and businesses that lined the route had a hollow feeling to them. Hardly anyone was outside. The few people he saw were solemn or long-faced as they went about their business. He noted that the community watering hole with the loud sign, Arroyo Saloon, was closed.

An old man in a rocking chair under a roofed porch sullenly watched him ride by. Ben felt the man's cold stare follow him down the street. Going in the opposite direction, an empty buckboard creaked past him. The glum driver, who was mumbling something to himself, never looked in Ben's direction. Echoing off the buildings was the distant clanking of a blacksmith's hammer rhythmically striking something on an anvil. Its sound rang clear, unopposed by the clatter one would normally expect toward the end of day from a bustling settlement the size of Iron Horse Junction.

As he approached the center of town, a light wind carried the unmistakable scent of the recent fire. All he had to do was follow his nose to the burned-out hulk of the sheriff's office. The jail bars towered over a pile of blackened rubble. A loose cell door squeaked as it wavered in the breeze. Ben stopped and gazed over the charred remains.

"I reckon you're Marshal Ben Corrigan?" someone asked.

He nodded but didn't stop staring at the burned-out building.

"We've been expecting you," the man with the black bowler declared.

"Howdy," Ben said somberly as he turned to face the man. "That must've been one hell of a jail break."

"Oh, Marshal, you've no idea. This town is scarred for life."

"Do you know where I can find the sheriff?"

"I'm the sheriff. Well, actually, I'm the acting sheriff. I don't have a badge 'cuz we lost them in the fire. Our real sheriff is indisposed. You see, his nephew was one of the murdered deputies. He and his distraught wife are overcome with grief. They've been holed up in their house since the fire," the man with the lopsided black string bow tie pointed down the street toward where the Gibsons lived. "I'm Ted Neely, the town's undertaker, also fire brigade commander, spur-of-the-moment coroner, and now temporary sheriff. The town council drafted me on account of Sheriff Willy Gibson's sudden bereavement."

"My congratulations...I think," Ben replied as he dismounted from his horse. "Where are the other two marshals, Eddie Blake and George Whitmore? They're supposed to meet me here."

"Oh, they hightailed it out of here yesterday. Said they got a telegraph from Sheriff Charlie Watson at Apache Wells—that's the next town just west of here—that men fitting the description of them outlaws had been seen around town. Told me to tell you they couldn't wait for you, seeing that they had to get hot on them outlaws' trail." Ted forced a smile as he tried to say something that would temporarily change the unpleasant subject. "You know, it's amazing how that telegraph spreads the word."

"Ain't it the truth? Just a marvel of an invention. Now, can you tell me exactly what happened?"

*　　*　　*

"More coffee?" Ted Neely asked before he refilled his own cup.

"No, I'm good for now," Ben replied, noticeably uncomfortable. The acrid odor of embalming fluid hung in the air. He strained to ignore the unpleasant smell that penetrated Ted Neely's tidy office through the open door of an adjacent dark room.

Even though the building was a funeral home, Ted's office looked more like a lawyer's office. Pictures of Washington, Lincoln, and Jesus Christ decorated the chalk walls. Ted's mortician's license was proudly posted above a gigantic desk. Against the wall farthest from the door was a dark-blue sofa stuffed with horse hair. Small off-white and burgundy Persian carpets dotted the polished dark-wood floor. Near the Franklin stove in the center of the room were a sturdy rocking chair, a small stack of wood, and a small bucket of chestnuts.

Ted suddenly realized why the marshal appeared uncomfortable. "So sorry. I guess I'm getting used to the stink." He finished filling his cup, placed the coffee pot back on the Franklin stove, and hastened to close the door. "An unfortunate consequence of the recent upturn in my business."

Ben had experienced the repugnance of mortician preparations many times during his career. His job required regular contact with coroners and undertakers in gathering post-mortem information. However, the vapor from Ted's embalming room was overpowering.

"I understand," Ben said as he took a slow sip from his coffee, allowing his nose to linger over its aroma. "But to tell you the truth, a dead skunk has a more pleasant smell."

Ted chuckled as he flung open the three windows to his office.

The curtains fluttered as a gush of fresh air filled the room. Ben smiled at the welcome relief. "That's better," he sighed.

"Yeah, even I notice the difference."

"You know, I swear, I've heard of this troublemaker Jameson," the Marshal said thoughtfully. "I just can't place him."

"It wouldn't surprise me in the least. These murderers have got to be on somebody's wanted posters even before they came to our town. Anyway, that's the story. I've told you all I know. Do you have any questions?"

"Yeah, I want to question this Hank McCutcheon. In what direction is the Bar-Z Ranch?"

"It's just a few miles northwest of town. I can take you there if you like."

"Thanks, but I'll find it. You'll probably be needed in town." Ben finished the last of his coffee and put the cup on the small table near the mammoth roll-top desk. It was the biggest piece of furniture he had ever seen. The blonde oak glistened under a smooth coat of lacquer. A solid wooden chair of the same color with rollers complemented the desk. There were dozens of small drawers above the desktop. Each drawer had a brass pull and keyhole.

"Oh, I'm gonna have to talk with Sheriff Gibson," Ben said, "but I'll do that as the last thing before I leave town."

"Good idea. That'll give him a little more time to get himself together."

"Yeah, that's what I thought. Two more things: Where's the hotel? And where's the telegraph office?"

"Sadie's Hotel is next to the jail. She's got the nicest rooms in this part of the territory and has the best meals in town." Ted beamed a smile. He seemed glad to talk about something else. "The telegraph office is in the train depot located in the north part of town. You can't miss it. Just follow the train tracks. Incidentally, you can stable your horse and mule across the street from the hotel."

Ben nodded and carefully crafted a parting response. "For whatever it's worth, I'll catch these killers. I've been doin' this for almost forty years, and I've always got my man. They're not going to escape from my clutches. I'll bring them to justice and see them hung for their crimes. It's a shame this town had to endure what it did, but it's what I can do to settle the score."

"I appreciate that, Marshal. I'll make sure the word gets out. You're not gonna need a posse from us are ya?"

"I think not. I'll round up a posse from Apache Wells if I need to give chase. You people need to mend. That's more important. Have a good night, Mr. Neely."

"You do the same, Marshal."

*   *   *

Early the next day, Ben headed out to the Bar-Z Ranch. The comfortable hotel room and the tasty breakfast were just as Ted Neely advertised. It helped to mellow the dark mood that had settled on Ben when he had entered the town the previous evening. Before he left, he sent a telegraph to the sheriff at Apache Wells, asking him for any further news on the sightings of the fugitives and for the whereabouts of the two young marshals. He'd check for any response when he returned.

Exiting the town from the northwest, he followed a rough wagon-rutted trail that led directly to the ranch. In the bright sun of the day, it took him less than an hour to reach the ranch. A short, stocky man with a thick handlebar mustache came out from what appeared to be the main house and waited for him on the porch. He glared with large, round eyes at the approaching marshal.

Around the rundown gray house were several smaller weathered buildings and a large barn with a corral. They stood out in a landscape that had few trees and acres of knee-high grass. A number of farm-hands were busily going about their daily chores, oblivious to Ben's arrival. In the distance, he heard the cattle bellowing.

"Howdy," Ben greeted the balding man when he reached the porch. "I'm looking for Hank...."

"You found him, Marshal Ben Corrigan."

Ben flinched. "My, word travels fast."

As he started to get off his horse, Hank raised his hand to stop him.

"No need to get off your horse, Marshal. I'm a busy man. Get to the point so we can all go about our business."

"Well, that's not a very sociable way of putting it, Mr. McCutcheon," Ben shot back.

"I most likely can save us time by saying that those three bastards were nothing but hired hands to me. I gave them orders and checked on them from time to time, but never had anything else to do with them."

"What about the rest of your crew? They may know something about...."

50

"They also had very little to do with them. Those three kept pretty much to themselves. They ate together, bunked together, went off to the range together, and went into town together. They ignored everybody else."

"Just the same, I'd like to question your hired hands."

"Look, Marshal, I'm short-handed. I just lost two more men the day after the fire in town. They just dropped everything and left. I don't want my remaining hired help wasting their precious time giving you the same answer I just told you. There's a mountain of work that needs to be done around here. Now, unless you got some kind of court order, I'll bid you a good day, so I can get back to work."

Ben's blood had reached the boiling point, but he didn't want to inflame the situation. He forced himself to smile as he asked, "Just one last question. Out of curiosity, if these three men were so disagreeable, why did you keep them on?"

"Marshal, you really don't know anything about running a ranch, do you? Finding and keeping capable hired hands ain't easy. I could care less who they are. All I care about is that they do their work and cause me no trouble. That they did, and I can tell you that all three of them were the best cow punchers I've ever had. It's going to be hard to replace them. Now are you through?"

Ben paused, cleared his throat, and looked Hank McCutcheon square in the eye and said, "Until I decide that I need to come back with that court order, I think I'm done here."

Hank McCutcheon frowned and fumed before storming back into his rickety house.

Ben didn't wait to watch him slam the front door. He had Betsy heading back to town as soon as McCutcheon's head started turning a bright red. The last sound he heard as the ranch buildings disappeared over a small knoll was a shattering sound. The kind a vase or dish makes when it's hurled against a wall.

*   *   *

"So, you found us," Jameson said in a haughty tone.

"You weren't exactly careful in covering your tracks, and I'm an old hand at tracking," the husky man casually replied. "Shep and I picked up your trail just outside of Iron Horse Junction. We later lost it in a gully but then picked it up again a few miles from here." He smiled, stretching the deep furrows that lined his olive complexion and accentuating the whites of his eyes and his pearly teeth. He had acquired his leathery skin from the many years he served as a scout for the U.S. Cavalry and riding the range as a cowhand.

Considering Jameson and his two pals had their rifles trained on him, he was unusually calm.

Shep, a tall, gangly kid who sported a pockmarked face and buck teeth, was behind him, nervously shifting his weight from foot to foot while holding the reins of their horses. He wore a cowboy hat with a tall crown. Around his skinny waist was a massive two-gun holster bristling with ammunition and housing two large Colt .45s. The oversize holster circled his pencil frame like a doughnut wrapped around a finger.

The two men were herding cattle at the Bar-Z when another cowhand who had just come in from town told them of the jailbreak and the fire. They immediately abandoned their work, went back to the bunkhouse to collect their few personal belongings, and went in search of Jameson's gang.

"Gus, I told you we don't want any part of you and that measly kid who minds you like you was his pa," Jameson fumed.

"Let's be fair about this. You didn't find this abandoned shack by accident. It was me that told you about it. Just like I told you that the bank in Apache Wells was ripe for picking. Damn, you should be half way to California by now instead of holed up not more than thirty miles from the hornet nest you stirred up. You're broke and on the run. I knew you'd come here to rob the bank. Following your trail to this shack says it all."

"I ought to kill you right now."

"You need money. So do I. The more of us that robs that bank, the better the chances we pull it off. There's plenty of money in it for all of us. Especially, if one or more of us don't make it."

Jameson squinted as he processed the merits of what Gus said.

"Look, you told me you never robbed a bank before," Gus stated.

"Yeah, that's right. I never had to," Jameson responded.

"Well, I have. It ain't hard once you get the hang of it. I can help you in that regard."

"What makes you think we won't gun you down after we rob the bank? What makes us think you won't gun us down?"

"That's where we're gonna have to have an understanding—sort of like a gentlemen's agreement. We help each other rob the Apache Wells Bank and Trust, and afterward we split up. You and your gang go one way out of town, and we'll go the other. That has the extra benefit of splitting up any posse that comes after us."

"Mmm," Jameson replied as he lowered his rifle.

"Now, I'm nobody's fool. There's three of you and only two of us. I'd feel more comfortable if I go into the bank with two of you. That way there's no chance of us getting shortchanged, and the kid and whoever is left stays outside to hold the horses and provide cover. Remember, Shep is a crack shot. He's outdrawn two gunslingers and killed several more. I like having him watch my back. So, no funny stuff, if you please. Are we agreed?"

Jameson looked at Callahan and Bledsoe, who also had lowered their rifles.

"Well, it wouldn't hurt to have more of us," Bledsoe replied.

"Yeah, why not? As long as there's enough money for all of us, I have no objection," Callahan added.

"Okay, you're in," Jameson exclaimed. "We're obviously in a hurry to get out of here, so we plan to rob the bank tomorrow. Callahan and Bledsoe have already scouted out the town. There's a warehouse just as you come in from the south. We figure on setting fire to the bales of cotton piled up in the back of the warehouse just before dawn. The fire should rage for hours since there's a lot of burnable stuff in that old wooden building, and during the commotion we hit the bank when it opens."

"Sounds good to me. Shep and me are going to stay in town. How about we set the fire and meet you in front of the bank when it opens? I reckon around nine o'clock?"

"Okay. It's a deal."

Gus extended his hand toward Jameson, "Let's shake on it."

Jameson hesitated but then shook his hand. Both of them smiled, but beneath their veneers they each worried about a double-cross.

Gus didn't wait for Jameson to add anything else to their conversation. He put on his can-do face and proceeded to take charge. "Now, where exactly is that warehouse? Let's discuss the particulars of how we're going to pull this off."

# *Chapter 10*

"*The Apache Wells Gazette* printed the description of those three. Since then, people have reported seeing men that fit their description in the past few days in different parts of town," Eddie Blake explained to Ben.

"Any of these sightings by the good citizens produce any promising leads?" Ben asked George.

"Nah, they're all of the 'I think I saw them' type. Nothin' else," George Whitmore replied.

"Did Santa Fe telegraph anything about other marshals joining us?" Ben asked.

"Everyone else in this part of the territory is busy with their own law-and-order problems," Eddie replied. "We're it."

"If you ask me, the whole world is going loco," George declared.

"Hey, Ben, were you able to meet with Sheriff Gibson?" Eddie asked. "He wasn't seeing anybody when we were there."

"No, he and his wife still aren't doing so good," Ben said solemnly. "Seems he was real close to his nephew and blames himself for everything. His wife came to the door, told me she and the sheriff couldn't speak to anybody at this time, and shut the door in my face."

All three marshals sat quietly with their heads down as if in prayer until Ben reached into his vest for his pocket watch. "You sure the sheriff said he would meet us here at seven? It's almost half past seven.

"That's what he said. But he could be indisposed," George replied, lowering his voice. "We've been told about his problem with the bottle. He's probably soused. I wouldn't count on him showin' up."

"Can I get you handsome marshals anything else?" the pretty proprietor of Lil's Café in asked as she passed by their table with a pot of fresh coffee. "More coffee? Flapjacks? Bacon and eggs?"

"Thank you, but I think we're good here," Ben answered for them.

"Just let me know if there's anything else we can do for you," Lil offered with a smile and a gleam in her eye.

"Yes, ma'am. We sure will," an obviously smitten Eddie answered with a bashful smile.

Lil moved her coffee pot and lithesome figure to the next table of ranchers. All three marshals followed her every move.

She was obviously older than the two young marshals but still young and jaw-droppingly beautiful to any hot-blooded male beyond puberty. More than one man had accidently swallowed his chewing tobacco when she strolled by.

"My, she sure is pretty. I wonder if she has a younger sister my age," a fully absorbed George said.

Ben cleared his throat, plopped down six bits, and started to get out of his chair. "Well, like I said, I think we're done here."

Eddie and George didn't respond. They were busy eyeing the stunning damsel as she delighted men at yet another table.

Ben sat back in his chair. "Ahem, I think there's a law against ogling in these parts."

"Oh, sorry, Ben," Eddie replied sheepishly. "Thanks for picking up the tab. The next one is on me."

"Mmm. Yeah. Thanks, Ben," George said, still staring in Lil's direction. "You know I think we should search the outskirts of town to see if they were spotted coming in or leaving. Then maybe we can pick up their trail. Personally, I think they've ridden out of New Mexico. It doesn't make sense that they would hang around here, being so close to Iron Horse Junction."

"It's possible that they may have stopped here to stock up before heading out," said Ben. "But if it's true that they're still being spotted, then something else is goin' on. We probably need to split up and search for possible places where they might be hiding out. Maybe they think they're outfoxing us by lying low so close to the crime."

"You know, I never thought about that," Eddie replied.

"But are they smart enough to do that?" asked George.

"Maybe," answered Ben.

"Hey, there's Sheriff Watson," Eddie announced, pointing to a man of large stature passing by the front window.

Lil began her rounds again, starting with their table. "You sure I can't get you gentlemen something else? I've got cured ham as black as molasses and freshly baked cornbread that I know you'll hanker for."

"You know what, Lil, you've convinced us to stay just a little longer," Ben declared.

"Good. I'll get you the ham and cornbread."

"Whoa. We're really full from breakfast. We'll have to pass on that until later. But we'll have more coffee. Who knows? You may keep us distracted until lunch. Then I guarantee we'll be lookin' for that ham and cornbread."

Lil giggled as she refilled their coffee cups.

"Oh, you'll need to bring an extra cup for the sheriff."

"Sheriff?" she asked in surprise. She looked toward the front door and saw the sheriff. "Sheriff," she huffed in disappointment.

Ben was puzzled by her response. As she scampered to meet the confused-looking Sheriff, he could hear her mutter, "A cup? It'll take a whole pot to sober him up."

Lil greeted the large man with a tin star on his shabby black vest. She frowned as she pointed him to the marshals' table. While he stumbled to meet with them, Lil waved one hand in front of her nose as if she was trying to clear the air, and with the other gave a thumbs-down to the marshals.

Under a dirty broad-brimmed hat with a huge crown, the red-eyed sheriff approached them with a woozy smile. A bulbous nose and droopy jowls accentuated his puffy face. His rumpled clothes looked like he had slept in them for weeks.

"Howdy, gents," he said, fixing his stare on Ben.

They all stood and replied, "Howdy."

"You must be Marshal Ben *Flannigan*," he said, extending his hand. "I'm Sheriff Charlie Watson. It's a pleasure meeting you."

"That's Marshal Ben Corrigan," said a bemused Ben.

"Really? Point him out. I've never met him," the sheriff replied, looking around the room.

All three marshals froze, clearly baffled. Ben pointed at himself and smiled.

The sheriff laughed it off, "So sorry. It's been a long night keeping the streets of *Fort Apache* safe."

"Of course." Ben shook his hand, and they all sat. The strong smell of alcohol flooded the air as the sheriff breathed heavily. He reeked of body odor and spilled whiskey. Disgusted, the marshals sneaked frowns at each other.

Lil came by, dropped off the sheriff's coffee, and fled the scene.

"Well, any more news on the manhunt for those desperadoes from *Iron Pony*?" the sheriff asked.

"Iron Horse Junction. That's what we were going to ask you," Ben replied. "By the way, try the coffee. It'll take the bad taste out of your mouth."

"Don't mind if I do," the sheriff replied, not in the least offended. He took long sips, which eventually took the bite out of the repugnant smell from his heavy breathing.

"We don't know if Jameson and his gang are still in the area," Ben admitted. "However, Marshals Blake and Whitmore have received a number of unverified reports from people who saw men who fit their description—a special thanks to your town's newspaper for printing their descriptions. If these reports are true, then there must be a reason for these outlaws to hang around town. I suggest all businesses, especially the bank, take extra precautions until we can be sure that these men are no longer here. We'll need your help in searching the area around the town for places they could hide. If we don't find anything, then we gotta move on and track Jameson and his pals."

The sheriff put down his empty coffee cup and stared bleary-eyed at the wall.

"Who are these Marshals *Bake* and *Morewit*?" he asked.

"Sheriff, that's us. ... I mean that's us, excluding Ben," Eddie responded, annoyed.

"Don't you remember? We introduced ourselves two days ago," an equally miffed George added. "And we're Marshals Blake and Whitmore."

"Uh. Oh, yes. Of course. My apologies." His shoulders lifted in an awkward shrug. "So much has happened since I heard that *Iron Pony* burned to the ground. It's hard to keep everything straight in my head."

"Iron Horse Junction," Ben responded, trying to keep a straight face. "Yeah, we can see that. ... I mean, we can see that it's hard to keep everything straight. Can we talk to your deputies? I think they need to get involved. We're going to need all the help we can get."

"Good luck," responded the sheriff. "They're a bunch of well-meaning but worthless drunks."

"Okay, this time we're really done here," Ben declared. "Have a nice day, Sheriff. Let's go, Marshals *Baker* and *Dimwitmore*,"

George reached into his pocket and dropped a quarter on the table. Ben and Eddie took their eyes off the sheriff, who had drifted asleep in his chair, and curiously stared at the quarter.

"Ya gonna tip her two bits for our breakfasts that didn't even cost a buck?" Eddie asked.

"Yeah, well, she deserves it. I mean the extra coffee and all," George explained.

"The 'and all' what?" asked Ben pointedly.

"Well, you know what I mean," he said with embarrassment.

He pled his case. "I know it's a long shot. But maybe, just maybe, she'll be more inclined to introduce me to her younger sister, if she's got one, or a friend like her or even an acquaintance."

*　　*　　*

"How can such a drunken fool be sheriff?" George asked.

"Well, at one time, when he didn't drink so much, he performed his duty with more dignity," Deputy Cory Drake explained to the marshals as they paused at a crossroads just north of Apache Wells.

"Yeah, but how does he keep his job?" Eddie asked incredulously.

"He's really likeable when you get to know him and capable of performing his duties when he's on the wagon," Deputy Harvey McGee added. "I know it's hard to believe, but when he's sober, he's real smart, incredibly strong, and a crack shot. The whole town feels sorry for him 'cuz he's got no family and no close friends."

"That so?" Ben replied. "We'll just have to take your word."

The five of them had ridden out of town after breakfast at Lil's café. They planned to split up and search the countryside. Ben assigned each of them a specific location. Two other part-time deputies were to comb the south. while they combed the north, east, and west.

"My, it's sure a fine day," Ben said as he studied the clear sky looking north.

They stopped at the crossroads, and everyone took the time to drink in the beauty and serenity of the closest thing to a perfect day before heading off into possible danger. Thoughts of Rachel entered Ben's head as he weighed a future with her love versus more forays into harm's way if he didn't hang it up.

"Okay, everybody knows their assigned areas. Let's go. We'll meet at Lil's at sunset. Remember: If you find them, ride back to find the rest of us. I don't have to tell you not to engage them, because you'll be outnumbered and a sitting duck. Together, we'll pick up their trail if someone finds them."

"Hey, what's that black smoke coming from town?" Eddie asked, pointing south.

"I dunno. It looks like there's a...fire," replied Cory.

"From what I can judge in distance, it's coming from the other end of town," added Harvey.

The sound of a galloping rider drew closer as the lawmen stared at the plume of black smoke rising into the blue sky. It was Kelso, one of the deputies assigned to search the south of town. Gordon was the other.

He rode up to them and shouted, "The railroad warehouse is on fire. The whole building is one big flame."

"What the hell happened?" yelled Deputy Cory.

"Gordon and me were on our way out until we saw smoke from the warehouse," Kelso answered. "We went to investigate, and there was a small crowd of people gathered around this wounded watchman. The warehouse was entirely ablaze. Before he died, the watchman told us that two men set fire to the warehouse after they stabbed him."

"Did he describe them?" asked Ben.

"No, he died before we could ask him more questions," Kelso replied.

"Where's Gordon?" asked Harvey.

"He's helping to organize a fire brigade."

Without further delay, the six lawmen sped back to town.

\* \* \*

In front of the bank, a nervous Bledsoe and Shep watched each other and the few passers-by heading toward the burning warehouse. They held the reins of their companions' three horses. A few people were milling about on South Street, pointing and looking in the direction of the warehouse fire. Setting the fire had gone as planned with one exception. Shep and Gus had to overpower and stab a watchman. The unsuspecting guard had stumbled onto them as they were preparing to light their torches in the back of the warehouse.

"Damn, what's holding them up?" Bledsoe exclaimed as he removed his hat to scratch his head.

"'Holding them up.' Now that's a corker on account that can be taken two ways," Shep replied in his squeaky, high-pitched voice, followed by a laugh that sounded like a pig squeal.

Bledsoe looked at Shep with incredulity while putting on his hat.

"'Holding up' like robbing somethin' or somethin' that gets in your way and slows you down. Don't you get it?"

"Yeah, I got it," he answered, followed by "ya dumb son of a bitch" under his breath.

"I reckon it could also mean taking somethin' and holding it above your head," Shep added, followed by more squealed laughter.

"Okay, Professor. You win the 'sooey' award."

A gunshot rang out from the bank. Jameson, Callahan, and Gus emerged with stuffed saddlebags. They tossed them on their respective horses and mounted. Unsure of each other's intentions, they paused to eye each other. Their free hands hovered over the grips of their holstered pistols.

Three other men ran out of the bank.

One ran down South Street yelling, "The bank's been robbed! The bank's been robbed!" He caught the attention of the clutch of people who had been watching the smoke from the fire at the other end of the street.

Another had a shotgun, which he waved in their direction. The shirt beneath his guard uniform near his stomach was dripping with blood. The pain became too much for him, and he doubled over, grabbing the wound with one hand and lowering the shotgun with the other.

The other man, heavy-set with thick glasses and a teller's visor, had a small pistol. He squinted at the outlaws and fired willy-nilly in their direction.

The bank robbers mowed down both men. The shouting man running down South Street was cut down halfway up the street. The small crowd at the other end of the street scattered. Jameson and his gang, with their smoking guns still drawn, stared silently at Shep and Gus, who also had their pistols in their hands. Shep and Gus stared back. Jameson had a dark spot of blood on his left side, but it didn't appear to bother him. Before any of them made the next move, several men regrouped around the body lying on South Street, drew their pistols, and fired shots at the bank robbers.

The bank sat at the intersection of South and Main streets. Jameson and his gang fled west on Main Street. Shep and Gus went the other way.

Jameson and his gang rode like the dickens out of town without incident. Unfortunately, for Shep and Gus, they rode directly into the arriving six lawmen. Gus and Shep stopped short of the six riders wearing shining badges, who also reined in their galloping horses to avoid a collision. A rider trailing Shep and Gus shouted, "Get them! They just robbed the bank!"

Bedlam broke out as both sides exchanged gunfire. Gus and Shep abandoned their horses.

Gus ran to a saddle shop on one side of the street. The door was secured by a huge lock and chain. He grabbed a heavy wooden chair near the door and hurled it through the large storefront window. Amid the sound of shattering glass and gunfire, he hurriedly fired a couple of poorly aimed shots at the scrambling lawmen and leaped into the gaping hole where the storefront window had been.

On the other side of the street, Shep jumped into the open doorway of a general store with both pistols drawn. The lone person in the store was the unsuspecting proprietor, who had been checking a bill of lading behind a counter. Shep took no chances and gunned him down. He leapt behind the counter, hunkered down, and reloaded his pistols.

Outside, the six lawmen shooed their horses away by pointing them out of town and slapping their hindquarters.

"You deputies take the saddle shop. We'll take the general store," Ben ordered. The lawmen separated into their assigned groups and hustled to the respective lairs that held their prey.

At the saddle shop, Cory, who was the senior deputy, took charge and posted Kelso in front. He and Harvey raced down an alley next to the shop to get to the back door before the gunman found it.

At the general store, the marshals took cover behind a water trough directly in front of the store. Barrels and wooden boxes of apples, flour, pickles, and peaches were scattered to the right and left of the open double doors. In baskets hung from wooden posts driven into the street next to the walkway were other edible items of interest.

"We've got to get somebody behind him," Ben said as he stared at the empty lot to the west of the store. "That's if he hasn't already escaped through the back," Ben said, pulling his kerchief from his neck and wiping his face.

"You want me to go?" asked Eddie.

"Wait. Let's see if he's still in there," Ben replied.

Ben removed his hat. And with the barrel of his rifle he lifted the crown above the trough in plain view of the entrance. A barrage of bullets poured out of the doorway, tore the hat off the rifle, and flung it into a pile of horse refuse in the middle of the dirt street.

"Reckon I'm going to need a new one. Anyway, I never liked that hat."

"You could probably sell that one to the sheriff. It would go well with his horse-shit-encrusted boots," George replied.

Ben crawled to the edge of the trough nearest the lot. "I'm going around the back before he does. You two cover me."

They both nodded.

He took one last look at the ground he had to cover and sprang toward the side of the building next to the open lot. George and Eddie unleashed a volley of gunfire that blew out the large windows, exposing the dimly lit interior. Bullets from inside the store whistled by him and others blew away chunks of the barrels and stacked boxes on the walkway, occasionally sending their contents flying.

He reached the edge of the building unharmed and dusted the bits of apple and smears of flour off his shirt and pants. The gunfire on both sides temporarily ceased. Ben waved at his companions and, with his rifle barrel leading the way, headed to the back of the store.

When he reached the back door, the gunfire between his deputies and the gunman had resumed. The back door was locked. So, he fired two shots into the keyhole. The doorknob still wouldn't budge. He fired two more shots, which broke the lock. He burst into a small back room filled to the ceiling with stacks of merchandise and dove behind a stack of wooden crates near the back door. The windowless room was barely lit by the light from the open doorway leading to the main floor and the opened back door. The exchange of gunfire had once again stopped. On his belly, he peeked around the crate, scanning the room.

From beyond the doorway, he could hear the distinct clicking sounds of someone reloading the chambers of a revolver. In the distance, he heard a single muffled gun blast. The shot must have come from the saddle shop across the street. He was contemplating his next move when he heard the slight jingle of spurs approaching the doorway to the main floor.

Ben had a clear view of the doorway and decided to stay put. When he rose to his feet and took aim at the doorway, his boot brushed aside a tin pie pan. It clanged, and the footsteps beyond the doorway ceased. There was enough light coming in through the open back door to see a light film of milk in the pan. It was probably used to feed the cat that kept the store free of mice. He saw the tip of a gun barrel at knee level at the edge of the doorway. Whoever held the gun was crawling.

"Hey, buster," he heard George call out through the shattered window. "Your buddy across the street is dead. We've got you surrounded. Drop your guns and come out with your hands up."

Ben's face was heavy with beads of sweat. He had lost his kerchief somewhere between the water trough and the back room. He wiped the sweat with his sleeve. Deciding that he wanted to preempt the gunman's assault on the dark back room, he picked up the pie tin and tossed it through the doorway. Immediately, the gunman opened fire on the pie pan, knocking it towards a side wall. This caused the lawmen outside to resume their barrage. The hail of bullets drove the startled gunman, who no longer had the protection of the counter, into the back room, where he fired both pistols into the dark indiscriminately in all directions. The shooting from the outside ceased as the lawmen listened and tried to discern what was going on.

From his protected position behind the stack of heavy wooden crates, Ben pulled the trigger on his rifle. The gunman stopped shooting. He gasped as he staggered back and forth in the doorway, dropping both pistols on the rough wooden floor. Shep fell to his knees before hitting his face on the floor with a thud.

"Ben, are you all right?" Eddie yelled.

"Yeah, stop the shooting. He's down, and I'm okay," Ben called back.

The lawmen entered the store with their guns in their hands. Ben had turned the body on its back. He was going through the dead man's pockets.

"Who's that?" asked George.

"I dunno. But from what I recollect, he sure doesn't match any of the descriptions in the paper," a head-scratching Cory answered. "He's built like a snake on stilts. There's nothing in the *Gazette* describing anyone built like a rail."

"That's a mighty big gun belt for a string bean his size," Harvey commented.

"He's got nothing of interest on him," Ben declared. "We need to get him to Iron Horse Junction to see if anybody recognizes him before he goes putrid."

"We got us a photographer in town. He can take pictures of both of them that we can send to Iron Horse Junction," Kelso exclaimed.

"That'll do," said Ben.

"Yeah, we'll have our undertaker prepare them to be viewed in their pine boxes by the whole town," Cory added. "Maybe somebody will recognize them. Then we'll bury them in a ditch somewhere far from town."

"Okay, so, where are we?" Ben asked while examining a rabbit's foot, a couple of dice, a pocketknife, and other sundry items he had fished from the deceased's pockets. "What happened to his friend across the street? I assume you got him."

"Yeah, I got him all right, with one clean shot," an unexpected voice announced.

A surprised Marshal Ben Corrigan looked up from his kneeling position next to the corpse to discover Sheriff Charlie Watson holstering his pistol with a smile of satisfaction. He was sober but still untidy in appearance.

"Surprised?" the sheriff asked Ben.

"Well, maybe just a little."

"I know every nook and cranny in this town—he cellar door to Hank's Saddle Shop in particular."

"Well done," Ben replied as he looked at the deputies, who nodded in acknowledgment of the sheriff's valor.

"All I had to do was make my way up the flimsy stairs to the main floor, find the varmint who was behind a pile of worn saddles staring out the busted window, and plug him in the back," the sheriff said. "I just got through hauling his body out front and talking to the good citizens who retrieved their horses and your horses."

"Much obliged," Ben responded. "That makes two down with one still on the loose. I wonder if one of these two is Jameson?"

"Ahem, Marshal, I got news for you," the sheriff interrupted. "Five men robbed the bank, not three. Three of the bank robbers rode west on Main Street. Two of them rode east. The three that went west made it out of town. These here men had the bad luck of riding into your path."

"But...."

"Don't take my word for it. The few people in the bank that I talked to before coming here said three men came in while two waited outside holding their horses.

"Then a couple of men joined the Jameson gang to rob the bank," Ben concluded.

A small crowd had gathered outside—most of the town was engaged in putting out the warehouse fire. They kept their distance from the saddle shop and general store, craning their necks to find out what happened.

"John Wilson is dead behind the counter," Cory announced.

The Sheriff heaved a sigh and pushed his hat above his forehead.

"That means we lost five good citizens to that mangy bunch," the Sheriff whispered. "Starting with *Iron Pony,* they're leaving a trail of death and destruction behind them. Maybe we should call up the army. This is turning into a war."

"There's going to be a day of reckoning for them," Ben said with conviction. "Right now, I gotta send a telegraph to Santa Fe, letting them know the bank was robbed by the Jameson gang of five, not three, and there's still three of them on the loose. I'll ask them for more help, since this is getting way out of control."

Ben turned to the two young marshals. "Let's collect the horses, check out of the hotel, and follow their tracks pronto.

# *Chapter 11*

Kristoffer Svendsen slapped the pencil on the bank document he was reviewing. He leaned back in his plush high-back chair and gazed out the window of his office into the fading daylight. The bank had been closed for hours, and he had been the only one in the building for the past hour. Frustration gripped him with an iron claw. For years he had patiently, politely, and courteously courted Henry Langford's widow, fending off all suitors until he realized that she was smitten with her sister's widower. "What does she see in this *sal boms* (saddle bum), Marshal Ben Corrigan?" he thought to himself. It was the nagging question that plagued him whenever he would so much as catch a glimpse of her or when his mind aimlessly drifted into thinking about her captivating charm. "What does it take to win this fine catch from this unworthy *stakkar* (wretch)?" He hadn't seen Rachel for a while. Bumping into her this morning fanned the repressed embers of desire that he had borne for so long into a raging range fire. He closed his eyes, grit his teeth, and slammed his fists on the desk.

Kristoffer enjoyed his perceived elevated status as the president and owner of Millbrook's only bank. He was undoubtedly the wealthiest man in town. He had the nicest clothes, horses, carriages, and servant-filled home in this part of New Mexico. Even though he was middle-aged, he carried a sturdy handsomeness on his six-foot-four frame.

"What a catch I am—especially to a woman the caliber of Rachel" kept playing in his head, occasionally interrupted by a chorus of "I'm tired of standing by, letting this *boms* have his way with her. I deserve her, and she deserves me. I'm the first citizen here. She's the town's first lady."

He reached for the bottle of brandy on his desk and half-filled a small drinking glass. The fragrant sweetness from the first sip was a welcome distraction. As he rubbed the glass back and forth between his large hands, a feeling of determination and resolve germinated. By the time he swallowed the last drop, it was in full blossom.

"I'm not going to stand by and watch this fine woman make a fool of herself any longer. She's making a mistake with that *boms*. I must make her see that I'm the better man," he said aloud.

He jumped from his chair, put on his hat, marched out of the bank, and locked the heavy oak entrance doors. A twinge of arousal produced a smile as he imagined the ecstasy of sharing the marital bed with his *vakker premie* (beautiful prize).

He had yet to formulate a plan to accomplish this. He couldn't think anymore because at moments like this a sensation, which he never failed to suppress, overcame him. Instead of taking a step toward home, he strode cheerfully in the opposite direction to the bordello above Millbrook's busiest saloon, Gentleman Jim's Watering Hole. He hoped his two favorite paramours were available because he couldn't think of anyone else with whom he would like to celebrate his newly found resolution.

*   *   *

The next day, Rachel decided to head to the general store to restock her nearly empty pantry, the result of her sons' and their families' hearty appetites the previous weekend. They had had a wonderful time together. Her grandchildren had grown at least an inch since the last time she saw them. They played for hours with a hoop rolled down the street with a stick. Her sons and daughters-in-law looked happy. They had thoroughly enjoyed each other's company. Everyone was healthy. When they were together at mealtimes, they had engaged in cheerful conversation. In the evening, they had sung tunes, accompanied by her sons' guitars. It had been a welcome diversion from her preoccupation with Ben.

Dark clouds had rolled in overnight. It looked like it was going to rain. She donned her rain cap with the big ribbon on the crown and the ankle-length raincoat with the dainty shoulder pleats—the kind the ladies wore back east. Tender thoughts of Ben crept into her mind. The way he brushed back her hair after lovemaking. His soothing voice as he spoke to her affectionately. The soft, warm, rousing way he kissed her. She missed him. Before she allowed herself to slip into gloomy thoughts about their unresolved relationship and his absence, she grabbed her basket and scurried out the door, hoping to beat any downpour.

Kristoffer had left home to start his day at the bank, still fired-up with the resolve to set things right with Rachel. When he saw Rachel, it was a serendipitous opportunity he couldn't have planned any better and a good omen. He made a beeline for her. She almost ran into him as he dashed in front of her on the plank sidewalk in front of the town's barbershop.

"Good morning, Rachel. Nice to see you this cloudy morning," he said as he tipped his hat.

"Oh, good morning, Mr. Svendsen," she replied, somewhat startled. "My, we seem to be running into each other a lot lately."

"To my good fortune, you add sunshine to a day like today. I must say, that's a pretty outfit you have on. It makes you look so elegant."

Rachel flashed a smile. She was accustomed to Kristoffer's unctuous comments. These particular compliments had a special flair that resonated with an ulterior motive.

"Well, aren't you nice?" she replied, hoping he would get to the point.

"I'd like to talk to you about some new bond issues that have been brought to my attention—I've invested not only money from the bank, but also my own money—when it's convenient for you," he exclaimed. "I've looked them over, and they will produce a handsome return."

"Well, I don't know," she responded. "I'm quite satisfied with the way my money is being handled. I'm not sure that it's necessary for…."

"I'm thinking about how the extra money can benefit you and your sons," he interrupted. "It would be something I'm sure Henry would certainly want. As his close friend, I want to make sure that I do all I can for your financial security."

"Thank you, Mr. Svendsen. You've been very good to us," she responded.

"It's always been my pleasure," he said, bowing slightly.

"But do I really need to look into additional investments, since what you've done so far has proven to be more than adequate?"

"Just yesterday, your son George applied for a loan to build a new barn. Extra money from an investment in short-term bond issues could pay off his loan early. It would ease your sons' financial burden of raising their growing families, as well as creating a bigger cushion for you, should there be an emergency requiring a huge amount of money. Believe me, I'm thinking of your overall welfare, as Henry would expect from me."

The sensibility of Kristoffer's argument gave Rachel pause. Having additional resources to handle life's uncertainties, as well as anything that would financially help her family, proved tempting.

"Well, I guess it wouldn't hurt to look into it."

"Good. May I meet with you at the bank this evening?"

"This evening?" she questioned.

"Say, close to five, so I will be finished with the day's business and can give you my fullest attention," Kristoffer said with eagerness.

"I suppose this evening would be okay," she agreed impulsively out of friendship.
Rachel was surprised that he wanted to meet so soon. But since she had no obligations that evening, she agreed.

\*   \*   \*

"Ah, a good evening, Rachel," Kristoffer said, running to greet her as she walked into the bank.

"Good evening, Mr. Svendsen," she replied, looking about the bank. She smiled and waved at the people she knew. Rachel was predisposed to reject any other financial pursuits. But out of courtesy and a little curiosity as to what he was going to propose, she had decided to come. After all, he had been her friend and trusted money advisor since Henry's passing.

She had spent the rest of her day cleaning up the stable behind her home in some loose blouse and britches. A ponytail poked out behind a straw hat that kept bits of hay from getting caught in her scalp. She debated whether to freshen up and change before her meeting with Kristoffer but decided that she wanted to allay any renewed interest he had been recently exhibiting. So she elected to stroll to the bank in her present attire, minus the hat. The rain that took up the greater part of the day had stopped, and the clouds had disappeared. It turned out to be a beautiful evening. She headed to the bank, hoping to conclude this matter as quickly as possible.

When she arrived, Kristoffer was speaking with a customer at a teller station. He greeted her and asked her to wait in his office. Jerome, the senior clerk and a good friend of hers, led her to a comfortable chair in front of a large desk. A little after five o'clock, Kristoffer walked in, closed the door, took her hand in greeting, and sat behind his desk.

"Please forgive me. I'm sorry for the delay, but Ralph Klinger wanted to apply for a loan to purchase a large quantity of barbed wire. I had to draft the agreement, explain it to him, and give him the money. It took a little longer than I expected."

"I understand," she responded and then offered him a compliment equal to a typical Svendsen embellishment. "You seem to always be there to help our community. It's something we in this town appreciate."

"Well, that's my job as a good banker and a good citizen. I'm proud to help where I can."

Rachel nodded, anxiously waiting for Kristoffer to get on with the investment opportunities he said would benefit her. She wanted to get home to supper.

"Yes, well, let's get down to business," he said as he pulled some paperwork out of his desk drawer. "I'm really excited about some outstanding opportunities that I'm sure you'll find are exceptional investments and will add to your personal fortune. They are capable of producing a substantial return." He gripped the documents so tightly in his big hands that there were noticeable creases where he held them. "There's a silver-mining operation in Colorado being undertaken by the Rocky Mountain Drilling Company. They're looking for more capital to expand...."

There was a knock at the door.

"Come in," Kristoffer shouted with annoyance.

"Sorry for the interruption," Jerome apologized. "We're done for the day. Do you want me to lock up as we leave?" the diminutive man with spectacles at the end of his long nose asked.

"Yes, Jerome. Have a nice evening, and I will see you tomorrow," Kristoffer responded in a civil tone.

"Very good. Good night, sir. Good night, Rachel," he replied.

"Have a good night, and please say hello to Millie for me," Rachel replied, referring to Jerome's wife, of whom she was fond.

"Thank you. I will," he said before leaving and closing the door.

Kristoffer continued his spiel about the mining company's bond issue and then proceeded to discuss the town's ambitious project to build a new elementary school, which also required a bond issue. They could hear the shuffling of feet and friendly banter outside his office as the employees filed out of the bank. Then there was the echo of the bank doors closing and the clinking sound of the doors being locked. What followed was absolute silence, with the exception of the drone of Kristoffer's voice, which started to waver. It was at this point that Rachel noticed beads of sweat forming on his brow and that his cheeks had a twinge of blush.

This was the moment he had been waiting for—all these years. But the big question was how to raise the delicate subject of his superiority as the prime suitor and show her the error of her ways. The bank was empty, so any raised voices in a spirited discussion would go unnoticed. He had never done this before, was unsure how to proceed, and knew that her reaction would be hostile. His uncertainty was getting the better of him.

"As you can see...my dear...these bonds are solid...quite safe and secure. I highly recommend that...."

"Mr. Svendsen, are you not feeling well?" she asked with growing concern.

"Please, call me Kristoffer," he said gently as he released his grip on the documents, allowing them to fall to the desk. "Haven't we known each other well enough all these years? By this time, we should be on a first name basis, my dear Rachel. When you address me by my last name, it keeps us at a distance—distance that you have been trying to maintain since you started your affair with Ben Corrigan."

A satisfied smile crossed his face as he stared at Rachel, relieved that he finally had broached the subject.

"How dare you!" she replied with indignation as she jumped up from her chair. She marched to the door and hurled it open.

"Rachel, I'm not done talking with you. Please come back so we can discuss this like intelligent people," he called after her. "You will see that you are not sensible in your choice of a companion. I'm so much more the man than that *boms*." This was not the situation he was expecting. She was supposed to remain seated and listen as he masterfully refuted all her arguments.

She reached the thick wooden front doors and tried in frustration to turn the locked handle. Flustered, she swung around to face Kristoffer, who was standing at the doorway to his office, and demanded that he unlock them. He leaned against the doorjamb of his office door and grinned at her impetuousness. Now that he had made his righteous intentions known, he sprang ahead to tame this shrew.

"Unlock these doors," she demanded.

"Not 'til I say something I've been wanting to say for a long, long time," he replied firmly.

"I don't want to hear anything you have to say. Let me out of here or I'll...."

"Scream," he finished as he walked toward her.

Rachel understood that something was going terribly wrong. A conversation with a man she had known for years as well-mannered was unraveling into something dreadful. For the first time ever, she saw something demonic in his narrowed eyes.

"Don't you dare come near me," she shouted and pointed at him.

He stopped and broke into what he thought was a friendly smile. To Rachel, it was a menacing leer.

"Why have you rejected me over that *boms* who destroyed your sister? When it comes to the best man, I don't see how he comes close. Why can't you see that? He has cast a spell on you like he did to your sister. It, too, will destroy you. I cannot stand by any longer and watch that happen. Henry would never forgive me if I did."

"You're crazy.... I mean, you're not yourself, Mr. Svendsen...Kristoffer. You know Henry wouldn't want you to treat me this way. Now, come to your senses and unlock these doors so I can go home before you do something we're both going to regret," she pleaded, trying to reason with him.

He took a couple more steps until Rachel let out a shriek.

"You fear me? All these years, I have been a perfect gentleman to you. All these years, I've waited for you to come to your senses. All these years, I've endured utter humiliation as the first man in town rejected by its finest lady. Now you fear me?"

His expression changed to dejection.

"I've never, ever humiliated you," she replied. "I've always held you in respect until now. The whole town knows that I consider you a good friend. My relationship with Ben has nothing to do with you. My personal life is no concern to you, as your personal life is no concern to me."

"It's got to stop," he stated ominously as he advanced toward her.

Rachel lunged away from the door to a nearby desk that had a large letter opener in plain view on the desktop next to a stack of correspondence waiting to be opened. It was fashioned to look like a dagger, which it could have been. She snatched it and pointed the shiny blade's tip at Kristoffer.

"Unlock these doors and open them," she commanded. "I don't want you to just unlock the doors. I want you to open both double doors so I can see the street, and then I want you to move away. You're in trouble now, but you'll be in worse trouble if you lay a hand on me. What do you think Ben and my sons will do to you when they find out? What do you think the whole town will do to you?"

Kristoffer looked at the letter opener with a scowl.

"Very well," he said as he went to the solid oak doors, unlocked them with a large key from his pocket, took a few steps away from the doors, and looked at Rachel.

"Why didn't you open up the doors like I told you?" she asked with suspicion.

Kristoffer didn't answer. His scowl was replaced by a blank expression.

"Open up the doors and stand aside," she ordered.

He stood motionless, staring at her.

"Did you hear what I said? Open the doors so I can walk straight out of here and then stand aside," she shouted.

He continued to stand motionless, gazing at her.

Rachel gasped. She looked between Kristoffer and the doors, wondering what she should do.

Slowly, she moved toward the doors, pointing the silver blade of the letter opener at him. He calmly watched her and didn't make a move.

When she got to the doors, she grasped the doorknob and found it still locked. In a sleight of hand, Kristoffer had unlocked and relocked the doors.

When she shrieked in disappointment, he leaped at her, extending his arms to grab the hand holding the letter opener.

A struggle ensued, but she was no match for the huge Kristoffer Svendsen. He grabbed and twisted her hand. She dropped the letter opener with a clunk. He knocked her down and fell on top of her.

"Threaten me, will you? I'll tell everyone you came here and willingly made love to me. The whole town knows of your scandalous relationship with that *sal boms*. What makes you think they haven't suspected that you were loose with me and Winkelman before your romance with Ben? What makes you think they haven't suspected that we have been intimate when Ben is away?"

Kristoffer's rage abruptly shifted into wanton desire as he realized that he, at last, had her soft, supple body pinned beneath him. His restrained lust burst to life. He released her hands and ripped her blouse, exposing her pink breasts. A fire ignited in his loins. The result was to unleash pent-up, blind, passionate fury.

She yelled and pounded him with clenched fists. He didn't even flinch, absorbing the blows to his prize-fighter-toughened side and back as if nothing was striking him at all. Exhausted, she dropped both arms to the floor as she squirmed to resist his efforts to pull her britches down with one hand and release his stiff manhood with the other.

With all the energy she could muster, she weaved on her back in a futile attempt to escape. The few inches of movement brought the back of her right hand in contact with the cold handle of the dagger-like letter opener. As he forced her to yield, she grabbed the handle and plunged the letter opener into his side.

He cut loose a bloodcurdling scream. He rolled off Rachel and landed on his left side, where the letter opener was buried. It pushed the remaining part of the blade farther into his body, up to the hilt. He gave another loud cry and flopped onto his back.

Kristoffer looked down at the handle emerging from an oozing crimson stain with horror. He gave a couple of groans and looked at Rachel with sorrow and regret.

Rachel was unable to move. No strength remained in her arms or legs. She heard him utter "*unnskyld* (I'm sorry)" before he closed his eyes and stopped breathing.

She inhaled deeply and struggled to her knees. With her hands in her lap, she wept, ignoring the pounding at the doors and the shouts of the townspeople who had finally heard the disturbance.

# Chapter 12

"It looks like they split up," Marshal Blake pointed out.

In a dry wash, a day's ride from Apache Wells, two sets of tracks veered north while hoofprints from a single rider went west.

"I wonder if they're trying to divide a large posse they think is chasing them," replied Marshal Whitmore.

"Well, we're the posse, and we're gonna have to split up," Ben said. "Too bad we couldn't get a sworn-in party together in Apache Wells, what with every able-bodied man putting out the warehouse fire."

Eddie and George had dismounted, while Ben was scanning the horizon from horseback. Eddie checked the tracks going west, and George checked the ones going north.

"Hey," shouted Eddie. "His horse has one hoof unshod. Look, there's no horseshoe on the left front hoof."

George moved to where Eddie was examining the hoofprint.

"Funny how we never noticed that before," George commented.

"Probably 'cuz his horse most likely tossed the shoe not far from here," answered Ben. "I'll wager if we go back toward Apache Wells a short distance, we'll find it somewhere off their trail. That's if it hasn't been thrown into the brush."

Ben glanced at the hoofprints but took more interest in the dark spots in the dry soil. The marshals had noticed occasional dried drops of blood, but in the last few miles the number of sightings increased and the spots were bigger.

"Well, whichever one is wounded, he's the lone rider going west," Ben observed.

"I wonder who shot him?" Eddie mumbled, thinking aloud.

"Probably that dead hero bank teller when he emptied his dinky pistol at them in front of the bank," Ben replied.

"Ya know," George exclaimed. "I've never seen a man wear spectacles that thick. He must've been nearly blind."

"I kinda wish we didn't stop at the bank to see what happened," added Eddie. "I never saw two men shot with so many holes. I wonder how long they suffered. I hope the Good Lord took them right away."

Ben rode slowly for a few yards, following the tracks heading west and noticing another group of dark spots in the soil. "He seems to be bleedin' more."

"How long do you think he'll last?" asked George.

"Hard to say," replied Ben. "It doesn't look like he's bleedin' to death, but it's got to slow him down. If he doesn't get to a doctor soon, he'll likely die of the fever."

Once more, Ben scanned the horizon.

"You two follow the tracks going north," he ordered. "I'll follow the rider going west. He can't last long if all this time he's been carrying lead. I'll catch up with you, otherwise you catch up with me."

George and Eddie mounted their horses and waited for Ben's final instructions.

"If you come across a town with a telegraph, make sure you send a message to Santa Fe. Offer a bounty to the townsmen, say the usual fee of twelve dollars for every man that joins you."

As they swung their horses in their respective directions, Ben added, "I don't have to tell you to be careful. So I won't. Good luck, and for God's sake watch out for ambush."

"Okay. Good luck, Ben," they called back.

*    *    *

Ben stretched his back and flapped his arms, trying to remove the tightness in them. Four decades in the saddle had taken its toll on every joint in his body. Luckily, he was still able to shake it off once he got moving. He had slept in a clearing near the Pajardo Creek sometime after sunset. The tracks he'd been following stopped here and then resumed their westward march just outside the clearing.

A recent campfire of blackened mesquite branches, spots of dried blood, and hoofprints of a horse missing a shoe indicated his quarry had rested here. There had been no smoldering embers when he arrived, but the ashes had been warm. The outlaw was hours ahead of him. He couldn't track at night, so he had bedded down, using the saddle for a pillow and the horse blanket to cover him. His thoughts had wandered to Rachel. How the heat of attraction burned hot between them. How they both complemented each other in every way. These thoughts continued into his dream as he slumbered.

As soon as the landscape became visible at daybreak, he watered Betsy at the creek, filled his canteens, saddled up, and resumed his quest. It wasn't long before the horse tracks converged with a path that came up from the south and headed straight west—the direction of the outlaw.

Betsy lumbered westward on the path while Ben chewed on his breakfast of beef jerky, followed by a couple of sips of warm water from his canteen. Thoughts of Rachel flooded his mind. With all the commotion since Fort Bascomb preoccupying him, he had been able to put any deep thoughts of her on hold for the most part. Now that he was riding totally alone, her image and their relationship took center stage when he wasn't focused on tracking his prey. In the solitude, his unfettered mind gradually crafted the choice he needed to make. It was here that he made an oath to retire to marry her.

As the morning approached noon, extreme heat rolled in, and the terrain became hillier. Every so often, a hot gust of wind swirled bits of dust around him. He stopped frequently to examine the horse tracks and the drops of blood that darkened the parched soil. Ever vigilant, he listened and scanned the vista for signs of his prey. Overhead, a turkey vulture glided effortlessly atop a current of rising hot air. For a few unguarded moments, he stopped to admire how it gracefully floated above him.

The outlaw, whoever he was, was heading into one of the most desolate parts of the territory. Ben knew that it was an attempt to get swallowed up in the vast uninhabited country. However, the outlaw's escape into a stark sanctuary was being thwarted by his horse tracks, which were plain as day.

A few miles later, the hills broke into piles of red, jagged boulders. He studied the path ahead of him. It wandered upward between two large clumps of rock. A lush thicket clung to the base of each clump—a sudden change in topography from the scorched grass and dried brush surrounding him. Sweat poured down from his forehead and dripped onto his shirt. He removed his hat to wipe his brow with his sleeve. The marshal took a long, steady look about, placed his hat back on his head, and reached for his canteen. Betsy lifted her head and made a sudden nervous whine, shifting to and fro.

"Whoa, girl," he said softly as he patted her neck. The mare stood still, but he could feel that she was tense. He took a second glance around him, studying the terrain for any causes of her unease. Nothing caught his attention, with the exception of the fugitive's horse tracks that went up the trail between the two boulders. Ben wondered whether the man was on his last legs from the loss of blood or the onset of infection. The fugitive had to be suffering the effects of his untreated bullet wound. It would be a blessing if he found that the outlaw had fallen off his horse and was sprawled out on the ground, unconscious or dead. Satisfied with his surroundings, he took a long, hard swallow of water while contemplating his next moves.

The canteen was knocked from his grip, and he heard the explosion of a gunshot. Ben flung himself to the ground and rolled into a deep ditch along the side of the trail, losing his new hat. Bullets thudded into the dirt within inches of him, kicking up wisps of dust.

When the shooting stopped, Ben was clinging to the ground with his pistol drawn, breathing heavily. He bated his breath and peered over the lip of the ditch in the direction of the gunfire. The thicket to the right of the trail was shrouded in white puffs of smoke. Between the smokescreen and the narrow angle, he couldn't discern the source of the gunfire. In the eerie respite, he slowly raised his head to get a better view. Then the gunman resumed his barrage, slamming lead into the barren soil around him. Ben responded with a volley of his own until his pistol was spent.

During the lull, Betsy, who had bolted back down the path, had trotted back. She stood a few feet from him, nervously pawing the ground.

"Good girl," he said, eyeing the rifle mounted next to the saddle.

A bullet hit the ground so close in front of him that it threw dirt into his eyes. He rubbed them furiously until he could see again. Brown tears streamed down his dirty face. After the next bullet grazed his hair, the marshal sprang up and ripped the rifle off Betsy.

"Go, girl. Get on outta here," he yelled as he slapped her hard on the rump. With a whinny, she galloped away.

All the while, shots whizzed over him as the shooter aimed too high. As Ben turned around to dive back into the ditch, a bullet tore through his left arm, causing him to cry out. It spun him around and hurled him to the ground next to a large rock just a few feet from the ditch.

Despite the excruciating pain, he crawled behind the rock. The hidden gunman, in frustration, unleashed a number of rounds, which ricocheted off the rock harmlessly. Ben yanked his left sleeve off and wrapped it around the wound, creating a makeshift tourniquet. It quickly became soaked in blood. He fumbled with it until it slowed the bleeding. He made a crude knot, using his teeth and right hand to hold it in place.

The gunshots had stopped while he had worked on the tourniquet. Ben wondered whether the shooter was sneaking up on him or moving into a better position. From the thick leather scabbard on his belt, he pulled out his hunting knife and raised the shiny blade above the top of the rock. In a torrent of rapid shots, the knife was knocked out of his hand.

Peeking around the rock at ground level, he could see that fresh puffs of smoke had come from the same thicket at the base of the boulder to the right of the path. His quarry had not moved. Providence shifted Ben's way when he spotted the black barrel of a rifle poking out of the undergrowth in his direction—allowing him to pinpoint his target.

A renewed spasm of pain caused the marshal to close his eyes and groan. He worried that he was going to pass out and lose the opportunity to slay the gunman. With resolve, he steadied himself. The new rush of determination propelled him to find the means to cock the lever of his deadly accurate Winchester rifle despite his mangled left arm. Taking careful aim, Ben squeezed the trigger, releasing a thunderous blast.

A piercing scream came from the thicket as the gunman tossed out his rifle. The shooter, doubled over in agony, tumbled out of the brush. Blood was dripping from clutched hands pressed into his chest. He stumbled a few feet and landed facedown next to the pitched rifle, raising a cloud of dust. The gunman moaned and heaved a final cry.

Hot, wounded, and exhausted, Ben lacked the energy to move. He gazed at the lifeless body of the fallen outlaw with satisfaction and relief. He hoped that Eddie and George captured the other two with less torture. Betsy had returned and, with low grunts, nuzzled him. Instinctively, she sensed her close companion was in distress.

"Betsy, my faithful filly. Always there, even to the bitter end," he mumbled.

In anguish, he rolled over on his back and made an effort to raise his uninjured arm to stroke her soft muzzle, but it fell short, dropping to his side. Then his thoughts shifted to Rachel.

"Well, Rachel, my darlin'," he mused out loud. "It seems both of our problems are solved. We're both going to be moving on."

The last thing he remembered was a ringing in his ears as he gazed at Betsy, who was whining and bobbing her head over him in front of a backdrop of a fathomless blue sky.

# *Chapter 13*

Rachel lay quietly on her bed, staring at the ceiling. The bedroom was warm in the late afternoon, despite the two open windows. Around the perimeter were the bureau, armoire, mirrors, accent tables, and other assorted furnishings that made the room comfortably Rachel's. It wasn't a large room, but it was big enough to also include her four closest friends.

"Your sons are on their way," her friend Millie said as she adjusted the bedspread around the edges of Rachel's bed. "Jerome rode out to tell them."

"Thank you," Rachel replied, gazing at Millie's warm smile. It was a true reflection of the honesty and concern within. It was what Rachel desperately needed during her lowest ebb since the death of her husband many years ago. Millie's strength came from years of coping with the hardships on the frontier. Her even-keeled countenance, molded by tenderness and a common-sense approach to adversity, made her a valued friend in the toughest time of Rachel's life.

"This is just the most terrible thing that's ever happened to our town," an elderly lady in a stiff dark-brown dress remarked. Her dark hair was woven into the fashionable bun hairstyle preferred by most townswomen in the West. Unmarried and well past her prime, she had a school marm look about her. With a whimper, she wiped her watery eyes with a white handkerchief.

"Yes, it is, Veronica," Millie said. "Who would have thought this would happen in our peaceful community?"

"To think that one of our prominent citizens would do such a thing," a young, attractive woman in riding britches added in anger. A broad-brimmed hat held by a thin strap around her slender neck rested on the upper part of her strong shoulders. When word got to her at her father's ranch, she rode hard to be at Rachel's side. Her pretty, pouting face glistened with a slight coat of perspiration.

"Well, he got what he deserved, that whoremonger," a toothless, white-haired old lady in a wicker wheelchair exclaimed. She had penetrating blue eyes that flashed a feistiness through her puffy face. Her hair was pinned tightly around her head. A light wool blanket covered her lap.

"Now, Cornelia," Millie countered, "you know what the reverend said. He's paid for his sins. We must forgive and pray for his departed soul. Isn't that right, Grace?" She stared at the young woman in riding britches.

"I suppose," replied Grace, not all that convinced.

"Mama," Veronica addressed the prickly old lady in the wheelchair. "I don't think we need to bring the vices of that awful man into our conversation." She frowned at her mother and threw a glance in Rachel's direction before returning to scowling disapprovingly at her mother.

"Mmmpf," responded Cornelia, undeterred, as she adjusted the blanket on her lap. "Heaven, Hell, and the whole town knows of his misbehaviors. Why, that den of harlots above that disreputable saloon would disappear if he and some of the other town's finest would stop frequenting…."

"Ahem, Rachel, do you want me to bring you another cup of tea?" Millie interrupted.

"Oh, I'll get it," Veronica volunteered.

"No, thank you," Rachel replied slowly sitting up in her bed. "I really don't want more tea. You've all been so kind. I thank you for being here." Her shaky voice rose, and tears dripped down her cheeks. "I just want this nightmare to go away."

The women looked at each other, unsure how to respond.

"Oh, Henry, why did you have to die and leave me lonely and unprotected?" Rachel wailed. "Why did Nora have to die and not be here to comfort me? Why did God take the two closest people in my life?" The room filled with Rachel's sobs.

"And where was Ben?" she murmured.

Millie pursed her lips and looked at the other women. She could tell that they had the same mixed feelings she had concerning Rachel's love affair with Ben. All of them knew and liked Ben, but as far as this relationship, they all had reservations after seeing firsthand what had happened to Nora, Rachel's sister.

"Rachel," Millie exclaimed, "please, you gotta get hold of yourself. You know there's not one of us that hasn't had to rise above hardship. You'll get through this. We're here to make sure you do."

All the women responded with a chorus of affirmation.

"'God works in mysterious ways, as we've all heard a number of times,'" declared Millie. "There's an Almighty reason for our sufferings, and I know in my heart it's to strengthen us for the difficult road we have to travel on our way to the Kingdom to Come."

Rachel stopped crying and concentrated on saying a prayer.

Millie looked tenderly at Rachel. "Now, I don't want to make light of this, but you have a solid reputation as a hearty member of our community. I know you'll rise above this. Think of how the good Lord has blessed you with two wonderful sons, daughters-in-law, and your grandchildren. We're all here to help you."

Rachel looked from face to face. They each returned a resolute smile. She sighed, forced herself to smile back, closed her eyes to continue her prayer, and wilted into the bedspread.

Grace marched up to her, clutched her hand, and said, "We're gonna get you through this."

# *Chapter 14*

"They're camped just ahead," Eddie reported.

It was the end of a long day. Both Eddie and George were saddlesore and dog-tired. It was their third day on the trail tracking the two fugitives. They were headed into the mountains, and the landscape became greener, with tall brush and weeds that provided excellent cover. The young marshals thought the two fugitives would elude them once they reached the rugged Sangre de Christo mountains. Spotting their camp was a stroke of fortune that looked too good to be true.

"My, they sure are dumb," declared George. "Why would anyone on the run stop and light a fire?"

"They should be hung for their sheer stupidity alone," Eddie remarked, shaking his head. "They obviously think they outran anybody following them."

Eddie had scouted ahead while George held the horses a safe distance from where the two men they were trailing had stopped to rest. A loud whinny from one of the fugitive's horses had alerted the young marshals.

"What do you want to do?" asked George.

"Well, it's gonna be dark soon," replied Eddie. "We can sneak up on them in the cover of night. They got a blazing fire going, so we should be able to see them when we get close."

"Good idea. But I have just one question."

"What's that?"

"Do we do the smart thing and shoot to kill or the not-so-smart thing and order them to surrender?"

"We're not bounty hunters," declared Eddie. "It's our duty to give the accused a chance to give themselves up."

"I thought you were gonna say that," George replied with annoyance. "Then maybe they're not so dumb. All they have to do is duck for cover and shoot at us first after we give them fair warning."

"Hush. They may hear us. Just wait till dark."

Shortly after all traces of daylight vanished, Eddie and George removed their spurs and crept up to the campfire with their pistols drawn. The fugitives must have turned in early. Two figures were tucked into blankets on opposite sides of the fire with their hats shielding their faces from the firelight.

As they got closer to the campfire, Eddie stopped and grabbed George's arm. The men under the blankets looked lumpy, and the fire blazed as bright as a signal beacon—too bright for men on the run. George could sense it, too. Ben's warning to watch for ambush flashed through both their minds.

Eddie pointed to himself and pointed left. Then he pointed at George and pointed right. They split up and circled the campfire. Eddie crept around the left perimeter, staying beyond the bright light cast by the fire. He was almost a third of the way around the circle when he spied a man crouched next to a mesquite bush and pointing a rifle in the direction of the campfire. The man had carelessly positioned himself within the edge of the fire's light.

Eddie looked around, didn't see anyone else, and snuck up behind the man. He pushed the cold tip of his pistol barrel on the man's neck.

"Drop it," Eddie ordered.

The man flinched, dropped the rifle, and raised his hands.

"Don't shoot! Don't shoot!" he pleaded.

"Where's your partner?" Eddie demanded, nervously looking around him.

"I dunno. He probably took off. Don't shoot!"

"You're lyin'. Tell me where he is." Eddie demanded, cocking the hammer of his pistol with a life-threatening click.

"Don't shoot! Don't shoot! I swear I don't know where he is."

What Eddie didn't see, George luckily did. The other fugitive left his ambush lair and ran toward the sound of his partner pleading for his life. He got close enough to see what was going on, unbeknownst to Eddie. The hefty outlaw started to raise his rifle.

"Drop it in the name of the law!" George shouted and then fired a shot at the man's left arm. The stout man dropped the rifle, grabbed his injured arm with his right hand, fell to the ground, and howled in pain.

Eddie was startled. He looked in the direction of the commotion, instinctively raising his pistol and pointing it at the man wailing on the ground. His prisoner spun around and knocked the gun from his hand, discharging a bullet into the ground. He cracked Eddie in the jaw. Eddie staggered a couple of feet and fell. The man made an attempt to dash into the night.

"Stop in the name of the law!" yelled George, who fired two shots at the man's running legs.

One bullet found its mark, sending the man tumbling to a crashing halt. He grabbed his wounded leg and thrashed on the ground, howling as loudly as his partner.

Eddie slowly got up, dusted himself off, picked up his pistol, and rubbed his sore jaw.

George sauntered over to him, the smoking pistol still in his hand.

"You're downright amazin'," Eddie declared as he stared at the two bellowing outlaws writhing in agony.

"I'm back to saying they're dumb," George proclaimed, "thinking they could fool us with that blazing campfire and the trick with the blankets. Who do they think they're playin' with, a buncha Eastern dudes? And then to top it off, getting shot after being warned? Yeah, they're dumb."

"Some warning," Eddie said sarcastically.

"Hey, not only did I follow the rulebook, going the not-so-smart way, but I also saved your life," George argued.

"I and my dear mother are forever in your debt," Eddie said with a smirk, "oh, mighty upholder of the statutes of the territory of New Mexico."

George smiled back as he holstered his gun.

"Now let's patch 'em up, tie 'em up, haul 'em to Santa Fe, and go find Ben," Eddie urged.

# *Chapter 15*

When Ben regained consciousness, he was in a daze. His left arm was in a sling, and it ached something awful. He was blindfolded and felt as if he was in a litter that was being dragged on the ground. He heard voices around him speaking what sounded like Apache. There was the clomping sound of horse hooves and the occasional equine snort. A strong odor came from the direction of his injured arm. He felt warm, so he pulled the blanket off with his good arm.

Someone shouted something in what definitely was Apache, and the dragging motion stopped. A hand lifted the blindfold. He squinted his eyes almost shut against the bright sunshine and raised his right hand above his face to shield them.

"Marshal Ben, it is good to see you awake."

"Blue Jacket?" Ben asked. The voice was familiar; he couldn't see the face.

"Yes, Marshal. I am Blue Jacket of the Jicarilla Apache."

"Where am I?"

"You are with us as we go to Tierra Amarilla. We found you hurt and fixed your arm."

"What? What's that you say? You found me? How did you find me?"

"We heard the gunshots on our way from the River Moro. We went to see. We found you and the big man you killed."

"The big man I killed...the big man I killed...the Jameson gunman," he said as he strained his muddled mind.

Blue Jacket knelt next to Ben and checked the poultice on the wounded arm.

"What's that sweet smell?" Ben asked. "It smells like...pine sap?"

"It is medicine for your bad arm. Your white man's God favors you. The bone was not broken. The bullet only made a hole in your flesh."

Ben tried to sit up. He was in a makeshift litter of animal skin stretched between two poles fastened to the back of a horse.

Blue Jacket gently grabbed Ben's shoulders and softly pushed him down.

"Rest. We will talk later. We have much to talk about. All did not go well at the River Moro. Our scouts saw your horse soldiers. There were many of them.

We left before we finished our ceremony. We left before the horse soldiers came and made war on us."

"You mean...."

"We avoided contact with them," Blue Jacket assured Ben. "We rode away. Like the fox, we made a wrong trail. They followed the wrong trail. They are easy to fool."

Ben didn't know what to make of this latest incident, but he feared the worst. "God help us if there's another Indian war," he muttered.

"Rest. Now you must rest," Blue Jacket ordered as he placed his hand on top of Ben's shoulder.

Ben felt faint. He closed his eyes, and his body went limp. Blue Jacket replaced the blindfold. It protected him from the glare of the sun should he try to look into the bright sky. It also helped to darken any light that penetrated through his closed eyelids.

A troubled vision of Rachel crying and wringing her hands flashed through his mind.

\*   \*   \*

Ben finally awoke from his restless slumber. It was dark. He was lying near a campfire. Blue Jacket and his braves surrounded the blaze, and there was lively chatter amongst them. Ben gazed absentmindedly at the fire. A tall brave holding a rifle saw Ben staring at the fire, went over to Blue Jacket, tapped him on the shoulder, and pointed to Ben.

Blue Jacket, who had been sitting on the ground eating, wiped his hands on his britches, jumped up, went to a spit over the fire, cut a large slice of the skewered meat, placed it in a shallow gourd, and went over to Ben.

"How do you feel, Marshal Ben?" he asked, putting his empty hand on Ben's forehead and squinting in the dull campfire light into Ben's telltale eyes.

"I reckon I'm okay," he replied.

"You do not feel hot," Blue Jacket said as he frowned in concentration and remembered the right term. "You do not have a fever."

He smiled, and Ben smiled back.

"That is good, and your eyes look good," he said with approval. "Here, eat this. You must build your...strength. Yes, strength. That's what the white man's medicine man tells us when we are sick." He placed the gourd next to Ben.

"Aren't you worried that the cavalry—the horse soldiers—will see your campfire?"

"Nooo," he howled. "We are going toward the sunset. They are riding the other way into the land of the Comanche. They do not know Comanche from Apache. They will fight the wrong people. The Comanche are our enemy. So maybe I am not right. Some things are going well."

Ben grinned.

"We are not fools like the horse soldiers. We have scouts outside camp watching for them...or others."

Ben chuckled, then grimaced at the shot of pain up his wounded arm. He caught himself and forced a smile at Blue Jacket. The cooked meat smelled good, and he was hungry. He grabbed the slice from the gourd and chewed on it with satisfaction.

"Tomorrow, you must ride your horse," Blue Jacket declared. "We must hurry to our reservation. We cannot be slow. Word will soon spread. We must be at Tierra Amarilla before Indian agent, our friend Mr. Higgins, finds out the horse soldiers are looking for us. If we are back and we have avoided the white man, he will stop the horse soldiers if they come to find us."

"Really?" Ben replied, not convinced.

"Yes...really," Blue Jacket assured Ben. "Mmm, new word," he mumbled.

Ben stared back, skeptical.

"Trust me, paleface. We have done this many times before."

*　　*　　*

Early the next morning, when Ben went to fetch Betsy, she greeted him with a lot of nodding, a cheerful whine, and a swishing tail. Ben rubbed her snout affectionately.

"So we ride again, do we?" he said happily.

The Jicarilla broke camp early. They helped him saddle and mount his horse. His left arm still ached, but the pain had subsided. Any thoughts of leaving his rescuers to reach the nearest town that had a telegraph vanished. He probably couldn't make it alone anyway. His left arm was useless. He'd file a report when he got to Tierra Amarilla. If the U.S. Cavalry caught up before he got to the reservation, he would vouch for them even if he had to shoot it out. As far as anyone was concerned, he was officially leading them back to the reservation. Since they caused no harm and were willingly going back, there was no need for military intervention.

As they hit the trail, Blue Jacket rode up next to him.

"How is the arm, Marshal Ben?" he asked.

Blue Jacket wore a large feather on his head, and his long black hair was braided and brushed his shoulders. He wore a beaded necklace and the tattered blue coat. His britches were dirty and his moccasins worn.

"Much better than yesterday. I think it's healing," he replied. "Now I know what a hawk with a broken wing feels like: absolutely helpless."

"You can heal at our village. I know Mr. Higgins would welcome you to his home. He is a good man and likes my people. We like him."

"He has made a favorable impression on me, the few times I have met with him. I'm glad he's still your Indian agent."

"My people would like your visit. The white man's medicine man often visits. He can help you too."

"Thanks, Blue Jacket. I may have to stay there 'til I can use my left arm to some degree. I'll talk to your Mr. Higgins to see if he could put me up in the stable. With his wife and five kids, I don't think there's much room in his cabin."

"We can make a tepee for you if he does not take you in."

"That's downright cordial of you." Ben struggled to find a word that Blue Jacket would understand. "I mean gracious...kind...good."

Blue Jacket grinned. "Core-jewel," he pronounced. "Hmm, another new word. Means good, eh?"

"Means real good," Ben replied returning a smile. Ben turned his eyes forward as he drifted back into thoughts of Rachel. The vision of her in anguish crossed his mind again. He must send word to her when he reached the reservation. This was his last mission as a territorial marshal. He had sustained the final injury his old worn body would have to endure in the line of duty. It was high time to settle down with Rachel. That's if she hadn't moved on.

# *Chapter 16*

In the cozy seclusion of the hayloft, Ben lay content. After a few days in the cabin of the Indian agent, Renaldo Higgins, the hayloft had proven to be more than adequate accommodation. It didn't have the comforts of home, but its simple solitude provided the perfect place for his convalescence. His wounded left arm healed quickly. Every day, it took less effort than the previous day to use his mending arm to climb the ladder into the loft.

Eight grueling days in a variety of terrain, especially the trek through the Sangre de Christo Mountains, had aggravated his injury. His arm had looked so bad when he arrived at the Tierra Amarilla reservation that Higgins had insisted Ben stay with his family for a few days.

Ben had laid out his bedroll in an unoccupied corner of the cabin where they stored nuts, flour, corn, and other foodstuffs. When Ben improved and was capable, he moved to the hayloft.

His interaction with the Harris children during his time in the cabin was something he would always remember as precious. All of them tended to him dutifully with their parents. Even the youngest would scamper to his side and go through the motions of checking his left arm. Ben would smile at her and give her a nod, saying she made his arm feel much better. She would giggle and run back to her brothers and sisters with a glowing smile. Later, when he was up and about, he spent time with them, telling the tall tales of his earlier days as a roving marshal. When he could move his left arm in front of his mouth, he delighted the youngest by showing her how to make a whistle from a blade of grass and cupped hands. He had pitched in to help around the homestead with his one good arm as far as he was able: gathering wood, hauling water, and tending to the livestock in the corral.

Mrs. Higgins, the Jicarilla squaws, and the reservation's traveling doctor finally nursed him back to good health. Mrs. Higgins's chicken soup and biscuits and gravy, as well as the fresh elk meat from the Jicarillas had as much to do with his recuperation as the medical care from the doctor and the poultice from Blue Jacket. He no longer wore the sling and almost had full mobility of his left arm. The dexterity in his left hand had returned.

As Blue Jacket had predicted, a patrol from Fort Bascomb had arrived, looking for the sojourning Jicarilla Apaches, and had left empty-handed. Since there was no theft, confrontations, or loss of life, Mr. Higgins assumed full responsibility for any disciplinary action. Blue Jacket and his band received another verbal warning.

He was approaching three weeks at this village of tepees, the single large cabin of the Higgins family, and the big barn with a corral. The landscape was more verdant than he remembered from previous trips. It was a pleasant lush mixture of short trees, low bushes, and tall grass. A stream wound its way through the village. Cooking smells rode the breeze from campfires that dotted the landscape, drifting through the open door of the hayloft and mischievously teasing his appetite throughout the day.

The pleasant din of the village's daily routine was his companion during the stretches when he rested alone. Resonating within the loft were the cheerful sounds of the Higgins children and their Jicarilla friends as they played during recess from the school taught by Mrs. Higgins. Their mirth mixed with the occasional barking dog, clucking chickens, crowing roosters, lowing cows, beating horse hooves, and voices echoing from the rest of the Jicarilla residents going about their daily business.

Most of the Jicarilla looked solemn when he was able to visit Blue Jacket. None of them looked distressed, but they were definitely unhappy. Blue Jacket had aptly described their prevailing mood. Everyone Ben met was courteous but reserved.

Blue Jacket's hospitality and warmth went a long way to cementing their nascent friendship. Blue Jacket's wife, Snow Eagle, fussed over him. Their three small children quietly eyed him from a distance with curiosity.

Within a day or two, he was going to leave for Santa Fe to submit his final report and retire. It was then on to Millbrook and marital bliss with Rachel. The day after Ben arrived at the reservation, he wrote a report of the events to the territorial marshal's office and a letter to Rachel letting her know that he was resigning his post to be with her always. He had received replies from the marshal's office but nothing from Rachel. He anxiously waited for the weekly, sometimes twice-a-week, dispatch rider from the governor's office in Santa Fe.

"Howdy, Marshal," called Renaldo Higgins. He had climbed the ladder to the hayloft and walked over to Ben with a broad smile.

"Howdy, Renaldo."

"How we feeling today?"

"As fit as a fiddle, thanks to everyone involved, especially you and your Mrs. Higgins."

"Yeah, she has a gift of healing, all right," he said in his slow deliberate manner. "Reckon she should have been a parson's or doctor's wife. Lucky I swept her off her feet first." He chuckled and sat on a bale of hay next to Ben, who was sitting up.

The tall, skinny Indian agent looked like he could have been a parson himself. He never left his cabin without his uniform: black wool jacket, white shirt, black ribbon tie, black pants, and black boots. He seemed to shun hats, Ben never saw him wear one on his full head of gray-streaked dark-brown hair, even in the rain or the bright sunshine. His bony, somber face with its scraggly beard was suited for issuing sermons on damnation, but it belied his true mild-mannered temperament and good-will-to-all disposition.

"Your reputation is the talk of the southwest, judging by the printed word in the *Santa Fe Times*," Renaldo said as he extended a rolled copy of the newspaper to Ben.

Ben slowly unfurled the newsprint to find his name splashed across the headlines.

### MARSHAL BEN CORRIGAN KILLS OUTLAW FRANK JAMESON IN A DUEL TO THE DEATH UNDER THE SUN

Ben had known it wouldn't take long for the U.S. Marshal's office to herald the successful elimination of the Jameson gang to the local press and to the newspapers in Denver, San Francisco, and Dallas and back East via telegraph. He smiled as he read the embellished account of how he took several slugs before killing Jameson. The account climaxed with:

> *Using the last ounce of energy that ebbed from his almost lifeless bullet-riddled body, the valiant upholder of law and order in this wild, untamed New Mexico Territory pulled the trigger of his trusty service revolver and dispatched the notorious outlaw Frank Jameson, a heartless desperado who laughed in the face of death as he spat at the marshal before he breathed his last venomous breath.*

Ben rolled his eyes at the miraculous recovery of this unfamiliar larger-than-life hero.

> *Then the severely wounded champion of justice courageously and painfully mounted his faithful steed and single-handedly rode into the sunset, coming upon a friendly settlement where the town's doctor worked feverishly through the night to repair his mangled body.*

He especially took delight when the article mentioned the heroics, with just as much hyperbole, of his two junior marshals capturing Jameson's two accomplices.

"Some yarn, eh, Marshal?" Renaldo said with a smirk.

"Ha," retorted Ben.

"It kinda reminds me of a story about this ancient Greek god-like fella named Achilles, who had an epic man-to-man fight with another god-like warrior named Hector. Except your account sounds a mite better."

"Yeah, I suppose so," he replied, shaking his head, "It reads like some fancy dime store novel from back East. At least they got my name right."

They both laughed.

"So this tells the whole world that you're the one who got Frank Jameson."

"That's what it says," Ben exclaimed. "My junior marshals confirmed the identities of Jameson's two pals before they were hung in Santa Fe last week. They promised to write me with the details of the trial and execution."

"Oh, that reminds me: I got some more mail for you, Marshal," Renaldo announced as he dug into a satchel that was slung over his shoulder. "It just arrived from the dispatch rider from Santa Fe."

"You mean he already came?"

"Yep, come and gone. You got some letters from the territorial office, Marshal Blake, Marshall Whitmore, and one from a woman named Millie Evans."

"Millie Evans?" Ben replied. trying to recall the name.

"Millie Evans from Millbrook it says here on the envelope."

"Millie Evans of Millbrook. ... Of course, I recall now. She's a good friend of Rachel, my intended."

"Mmm," Renaldo said thoughtfully.

"Thanks, Renaldo." Ben snatched the envelope from his hand and tore into the contents.

Renaldo chuckled as he asked, "I suppose you don't want to hear about the record-size bull elk that a Jicarilla hunting party brought down yesterday?"

Ben didn't hear a word. The excited look on his face melted into a frown as he continued to read.

"Well, I reckon not," Renaldo said to himself, knowing that this was the news concerning Rachel that Ben had been waiting for. He put the rest of Ben's mail on the bale of hay. "I'll tell you about it at supper. You are coming later to supper?"

Ben lowered his hands, gripping the pages of the letter. His wide eyes stared absently into a stack of hay at the other end of the loft.

"I don't think I can. I've got to go to Millbrook—right away."

*   *   *

"You really should wait until morning," Renaldo urged. "It's gonna be dark soon. You won't get very far."

"I can't wait," Ben responded in a resolute voice. "I'm gonna ride all night if I have to." He was frantically saddling Betsy with the help of Renaldo and his wife.

The Higgins' five children stood together, minding their good manners by keeping their distance from an adult matter. The eldest had her arm around the youngest. They knew something was terribly wrong with Ben and that he had to leave immediately to fix it. They could feel the distress and concern from their parents. Their eyes were glued on Ben, whom they had grown to like and respect. The youngest started to whimper.

"Ben, I know there's a sense of urgency," Mrs. Higgins said, trying to reason with him. "But if this Millie says your Rachel is recovering, what's the hurry? It's late in the day. Renaldo is right. You should wait until morning."

"I thank you for your concern, but tomorrow is another day when I'm not there to comfort Rachel. You...you just don't understand. This is all my fault."

"Fiddlesticks," responded Renaldo. "It's just plain bad luck, that's all."

"Honestly, Ben," Mrs. Higgins persisted. "You're still not completely healed, and you're putting more strain on yourself. Please wait until tomorrow morning."

"I'm so grateful to you all. I don't know how I am going to pay you back. I'll make sure the governor's office sends you compensation for all your trouble and expense. But this is something I just have to do. I'll never be able to look myself in a mirror again if I don't leave now. I...I just don't want to get there too late to help her. I just can't."

Renaldo took a deep breath. He glanced at his wife and shook his head. He glanced at his children and once again shook his head.

"Well," Renaldo said, "we can't stop a man who's dead-set on setting things right. Just don't push yourself too hard, Marshal. Sending us a message from Millbrook that you made it safely is all the compensation we need."

"Thank you, Mr. Higgins, I will, but you're still entitled to receive fair compensation. I'll see to that," Ben said as he shook Renaldo's hand. "I'll never forget what you've done, and I will always be in your debt." He looked fondly at Mrs. Higgins. "And thank you for your care and concern," he said taking her hand and tipping his hat. "Renaldo is fortunate that you 'fell for him first'."

Renaldo hugged his wife as she wiped her eyes with her apron.

"Here," she said as she slung a bulging leather bag over the saddle horn. "There should be plenty of jerky and biscuits to last you three to four days, depending on how hearty your appetite is."

"Thank you kindly," Ben said as he turned Betsy south. "So long, and please tell Blue Jacket I'm sorry to leave without saying good-bye."

"Godspeed," they shouted as he trotted away.

"Good-bye, children," he called back as he waved to them.

"Bye, Ben," they yelled in unison as the youngest grabbed her sister's dress and cried into one of the folds.

Into the late afternoon rode one determined rider.

# Chapter 17

"Ma, Fred Winkelman's here," Harry announced.

Rachel didn't respond. She sat quietly in the parlor with her hands on her lap gazing out the window into the town's main street. The town's residents were going about their daily business. She watched with envy. Oh, how she yearned to rejoin them in their mundane activities.

"Ma…Ma, Mr. Winkelman's here," Harry repeated, tapping her gently on the shoulder. "He looks mighty worried about somethin'. Kinda like a homesteader waiting to be kicked off his spread by ranchers."

Rachel frowned.

"He wants to talk to you about some important matter concerning your account at the bank."

Her face faded into a blank stare of confusion.

"It has something to do with the disposition of the bank."

"What's that got to do with me?" she replied, even more bewildered.

"Now, Ma, it must be something important," he replied. "The bank has to be in a God-awful mess. Fred's one of the directors. For him to come calling means he's got important news about the bank."

Her body tensed. She turned her head and resumed staring out the window.

Harry waited a few seconds and turned back toward the small foyer where Winkelman was waiting.

"Very well, I'll speak with him," Rachel said suddenly. "But I want you to stay here with me."

"Okay, Ma," Harry said as he went to get Winkelman.

Harry led the tall, slim lawyer into the parlor. Fred looked uncomfortable as he nervously glanced at Rachel. He had his black hat in one hand and a brown leather briefcase with a large handle in the other. He forced a smile and cleared his throat.

"Good afternoon, Rachel—Mrs. Langford," he said, probing her reaction.

"Hello, Mr. Winkelman," she politely replied.

"I do hope you're feeling better."

"What is it you wish to speak to me about?" she asked curtly.

His facial expression turned serious as he raised his eyebrows and said, "I know that this is a difficult time to bring up a subject that has to do with the bank." He shook his head and sighed. "But I must speak with you, since you're the bank's biggest depositor, about its solvency—for the sake of all who depend on its existence in this community."

"How am I involved in the bank's welfare?" she pointedly asked.

"I'm hoping your unfortunate circumstance won't cause you to move your money elsewhere. Many depositors may take note and withdraw their funds in a panic over the bank's creditworthiness. All the investors, including me, would suffer if there was a run on the bank causing a bank failure."

Rachel and her son quickly glanced at each other before refocusing on Fred.

"May I...may I sit?" Fred asked.

"Oh, of course," Harry motioned to the love seat to the left of the sofa where Rachel sat.

Fred plopped into the love seat, clutching his hat and briefcase as if getting ready to leave. He raised his forehead and stared into Rachel's eyes.

"It's tragic what happened, and I am sorry for you and I'm sorry for him," he continued. "It certainly wasn't like Kristoffer to act in such a shameful way. But as you know, he had his eye on you and felt slighted when you rejected him."

Rachel winced at this statement. Fred had also lined up with Kristoffer to pursue her. His detached observation only emphasized his shifty nature.

"No doubt his ego and boundless appetite for physical intimacy with the ladies finally did him in...ahem. Once again, I'm truly sorry," he continued as his face grew warm. "He has paid for his scurrilous deed, but the citizens of this town shouldn't have to pay for his misbehavior by losing their financial institution. So we, the remaining investors, have come up with a solution that should be most agreeable to you, the principal depositor, in order to protect the integrity of the bank."

"Which is?" Rachel asked with suspicion.

"Well, me and the other investors have unanimously voted to put you on the board of directors if you'll remain its largest depositor."

The silence in the room was deafening. No one stirred.

"What's that you said?" asked Harry incredulously.

"The contributions you and Henry made to this town and the bank have not gone unnoticed. Everyone feels your pain. It's the least we can do for someone so vital to the fabric of this community.

"Me, a bank director?" Rachel responded. "What do I know about the banking business?"

"You really wouldn't have to concern yourself about knowing the details of banking," he responded. "We'll take care of that for you. As a prominent member of our community, you would be welcome on the board to be a voice in the bank's operation for the benefit of the residents in and around Millbrook."

Rachel was unsure how to respond.

"When you're up to it, I can go over the particulars. For now, Jerome Evans will run the day-to-day operations until we elect a new president. You know him and his wife, Millie. I and the other directors will manage the overall operation until you meet with us to approve the new bank president just put forward by the existing board."

"And who might that be?" asked Rachel.

"Well, actually...they've nominated me," he said proudly. "I would very much like to assume the role as bank president to guide it through this difficult period, but I'll need your vote to make it unanimous. Under the bank's charter, it takes a unanimous vote."

She turned once again to stare silently out the window.

"Well, I should be getting along," he said, knowing that this new development overwhelmed her. "Good day, Mrs. Langford."

"I'll see you to the door, Mr. Winkelman," said Harry.

"Maybe you and I can meet to discuss this matter before the weekend, or sometime soon when you're able," Fred suggested with an eagerness in his expression. It was an unmistakable sign that he looked forward to the opportunity to renew his past avaricious pursuit of her. Staring out the window, she never saw his face, but knew by the suggestion in his voice that it was there.

"That's a big maybe, Mr. Winkelman," she snapped back, glaring at him with scorn. "From now on, my sons will take care of things when I need to deal with you. Say 'hello' to your lovely wife, Maggie, for me. We all hold her in high regard," Rachel said.

He hastily left the room. Harry let him out the door.

"Imagine that," Harry said, clearly astounded. "I can't believe it. That dirty scoundrel came here for his own selfish reasons. He's got to know that you can see through him. He wants to be the bank president. So he made you a bank director so you wouldn't ruin the bank, and he wants your vote. In the first place, why would you pull your money out of the only bank in town? It don't make sense."

"It *doesn't* make sense," she corrected and affirmed, not letting on her intuition that Fred had an additional motive of rekindling his pursuit of her money and influence. "Nothing seems to make sense anymore—not even Ben and me."

*   *   *

"I got real carried away last night and cooked up a storm," Millie said as she placed the basket on the kitchen table. She removed the cloth covering the basket's contents to reveal a plate of fried chicken, a bowl of green beans, several ears of sweet corn, and buttermilk biscuits.

"Thanks. You're all so wonderful." Rachel smiled, grateful for her close friends.

"As much as I'd like to," Millie admitted while removing her bonnet. "I can't take all the credit. Veronica and her mother made the green beans, and Grace cooked the corn."

Rachel stared silently at the gifts, so moved by their generosity that words escaped her. Her eyes misted with tears.

Millie grabbed her arm. "Honey, are you feeling any better?"

Rachel choked back the tears and buried her face into her hands.

Millie put her arm around her. Rachel dropped her hands and cried into Millie's shoulder.

"Now, I think you're coming along just fine," she said, giving her a big hug.

Rachel moved away to grab a handkerchief from her apron pocket. She turned away from Millie to wipe her eyes and nose.

"Has Reverend Childress come to see you?" Millie asked in an attempt to move on.

"Yes, he came," Rachel replied, obviously displeased. "He told me that I was being punished for my wayward affair, that I need to beg the Almighty for forgiveness, and mend my ways."

"Well, I declare. That coming from a man who has his own problems with the bottle and a wandering eye for the young ladies in the congregation."

"Oh, Millie, I don't know about...."

"No, no, we must call it what it is. Why, it's the talk of the church's ladies club. You've heard it."

"I knew the stories about his drinking, but I never paid heed to his attention to the young ladies. Even so, he's just an elderly bachelor dealing with his male tendencies."

"Elderly bachelor, my foot. He's been married. His wife left him for another man. I got it straight from Meredith, whose sister in Wichita knew him when he was their preacher. Well, he's been dealing with those tendencies a might too noticeable if you ask me."

"Why, Millie, that sounds like idle gossip. I thought you liked him," Rachel responded, somewhat surprised.

"I do. That man is definitely has the gift of the Gospel. His sermons are so rousing. But it doesn't take away what's obviously the other side of him. Don't take my word. Just ask Grace, Cornelia, or Veronica."

"I can well imagine what the gossip mills are saying about me and Ben," she said under her breath.

Millie didn't respond, embarrassed by how the conversation had segued into a taboo topic.

"It's no matter," Rachel continued, ignoring the awkwardness. "I know my romance with Ben is public knowledge. I expected the reverend's response. It's not something I'm proud of. It's not something that I wanted to happen, let alone become well-known. What it did was make me question my relationship with Ben." Rachel paused, closed her eyes, pursed her lips, and gripped the edge of the kitchen table. "That's why I couldn't write to him. I just couldn't."

"Honey, he had to know," Millie explained. "Somebody had to tell him what happened. You can't just not tell Ben that you killed a man in self-defense."

"I know. You did the right thing. I just don't know about us anymore."

# Chapter 18

Through the dusk and into the early evening, Ben followed the trail leading south from the Jicarilla village. He wanted to ride all night but had to stop by the side of the trail when he could no longer see anything in front of him. Under a crisp starry sky, he impatiently waited for the first glimmer of light in the eastern horizon. Betsy stood next to him and eventually dozed off. But Ben stayed up all night, sitting next to a tree. He gazed at the awesome twinkling spectacle above, contemplating the important chapters of his life, culminating with his present mission. In those nocturnal hours, his love for Rachel and his desire to be with her increased. It made it difficult for him to wait patiently for dawn. When he felt that he couldn't wait any longer and would risk riding into the black void surrounding him, the initial trace of daybreak crept its way into the eastern sky.

When there was just enough daylight to discern the trail, Ben mounted Betsy and continued his quest. Before noon he expected to reach the fork at the railroad town of Española and take the trail that headed southeast to Santa Fe. As the cloudless morning progressed, the traffic on the trail increased, with an occasional rider or wagon going in the opposite direction. At Santa Fe, he would board Betsy and take a fresh horse east to Millbrook.

It was late in the morning and Ben was within several miles of Española, when a rope was tossed around him, tearing him from his saddle and slamming him to the ground. Betsy was startled and continued down the trail in full gallop.

"What the Sam Hill is goin' on?" he shouted as he rolled on the ground attempting to stand.

"We got 'im," he heard someone yell and was hit in the back of his head, losing consciousness.

Two bandits pulled down their kerchiefs exposing their faces and quickly rolled Ben over, going through his pockets and removing his gun belt. A third bandit, who wore a tan hat with a huge black condor feather, stayed mounted on his horse, serving as lookout.

"Well, of all the rotten luck, this here fella's a marshal," a bandit with a scar on his left cheek shouted, staring wide-eyed at the silver star on Ben's shirt.

"Ya stupid son of a bitch, why didn't ya look before you roped him?" the other bandit, who had a bright red bandana, screamed.

"How was I to know who he was? Did ya see his shiny badge before I roped him? Did ya?

"No, but I wasn't the one doing the ropin'. You shoulda paid more attention before ya...."

"Boys, we gotta get movin'," the bandit on the horse exclaimed. "We can't worry about who we robbed. We gotta get outta here before somebody else comes down the trail. Get his gun and whatever else he's got and let's go after his horse."

The two bandits finished emptying Ben's pockets, retrieving his hat, removing his boots, and taking his gun belt. They placed all the contents in a large gunny sack.

As they scrambled to get back on their horses, Ben groaned.

"Hey, he's coming to," said the bandit with the scar. "Whadya know. I didn't kill him."

"Whoowee, that's the second careless thing ya done," responded the bandit with the red bandana.

"Aw, I'll fix that. I'll put a bullet in him," the bandit with the scar said as he reached for his holstered pistol.

"What? This close to town a gunshot's gonna draw attention," the bandit on the horse yelled. "You shoot that man, and I'll shoot you. What are ya, plumb loco? Whack him again a couple more times. That'll do him in. Then drag him out of sight into them bushes."

"Good idea," the scarred man agreed.

"Whoa, I hear somebody comin' up the road," the bandit with the red bandana exclaimed.

"There's men on horseback. Come on. Let's get outta here," shouted the bandit on the horse.

"Wait a minute. What about him?" said the man with the scar on his face.

"Never mind," the man on horseback ordered. "You cracked him so hard that I doubt he'll survive much longer. He's as good as dead. Come on. We gotta get outta here."

The two bandits on foot sprang to their horses. The bandit with the sack tied it to his saddle horn. The three of them took off into the brush, forgetting for the moment about Betsy.

Two drovers leading a herd of a dozen steers came down the trail toward Ben's sprawled body, which was off to the side but in plain view. They were working opposite sides of the herd, keeping them together and keeping them moving.

The young rider in his teens caught sight of Ben and did a double take. He looked across at his grandfather, who saw the body but turned his head forward, locking his stare past Ben and down the road.

"Grandpa, there's someone lying off to the side. Don't ya see him?" the young man shouted.

"Never you mind, boy. We gotta get this herd to market before dark. Keep movin'."

"But he looks like he's hurt. Aren't we gonna…."

"He doesn't look hurt to me. Looks like he's asleep. He's probably drunk and fell off his horse. Serves him right."

"But…."

"Hear what I say. We ain't gonna get involved in something that's none of our business. Come on. Let's move along. Yah!"

The older man waved and shouted at the cattle. The cattle and the horses hastened past Ben, leaving him in a shroud of dust.

The young man stopped briefly up the trail to take a long look at Ben's motionless body. A loud whistle from his grandfather snapped him to attention, and he rode off.

Sometime later, Ben drifted into head-splitting consciousness. The throbbing in his skull was so severe, he couldn't move.

A solitary rider came up the road going north. He was dressed in a white robe that matched his long, flowing white hair and beard. The donkey he rode strained to carry his large frame. If he hadn't bent his knees while riding, his sandaled feet would have scraped the ground.

He was singing something to himself when he spied Ben's body. Quietly he rode up to the still figure and stopped.

Ben saw him and uttered, "Help me. Please help me. I've been ambushed. I need help."

"What's that you say? You've been accosted by thieves?"

"Yeah…I need help."

"Mmm, do you hear that Barnabas, another sinner punished for his sins," the man said to the donkey, who, at the sound of his name, turned to look at the white-garbed rider and brayed.

Ben breathed heavy and tried to clear his throat as he struggled to ask again for assistance.

"What sins have you committed that you should warrant such a punishment?"

Ben frowned, clearly confused.

"Idolatry? Murder? Gambling? Drunkenness? Idleness? Adultery? Whoremongering?"

"Look, would you get me some help?"

"I am doing my part in rescuing your wounded soul, my wayward brother. By allowing your punishment to atone for your sins, you will be cleansed and will be allowed to enter the kingdom of heaven."

"What?"

"However, if by some miracle you should survive, then you must take this as a lesson to walk in the light and sin no more."

"Are you crazy?" Ben gasped.

"Godspeed to you, my brother, and pray for those who sin when you reach the great Jehovah."

The addled holy man departed, picking up his tune as he continued north on the trail.

For hours, Ben lay in the hot sun, unable to move. He needed water. Whatever feeble strength he had left was quickly leaving him. He closed his eyes and thought of Rachel, his failure to be with her in her time of need, his failed attempt to reach her to comfort her. Unless someone came to his rescue soon, he would die. His body closed up, so all the senses of hearing, feeling, smelling, tasting, and seeing disappeared into a black void.

In the realm of his physical detachment the last words he heard from Father Bonaventura echoed in the recesses of his foggy mind:

*"Remember, wherever you go, God goes with you."*

The words played over and over until they became a prayer, until he felt the splash of water on his forehead. Someone was cleaning his face with a wet cloth and was speaking soothing words to him.

# Chapter 19

"I tell ya. That's Ben's horse in the corral," Eddie insisted.

"You really think so?" responded George.

"What's he doin' here? We wrote to tell him we were on our way to Tierra Amarilla," said Eddie, looking puzzled.

"Maybe he never got our last letters," George exclaimed.

"Well then, it's a good thing we bumped into him here in Española. Let's find out where he's at," said Eddie. "We can take him to dinner and find out the real story about how he got Jameson. We owe him one, remember?"

"Yeah," responded George. "And we can tell him the real story of how we got Jameson's two pals and spent all that time patching them up, only to see them hang a few weeks later."

They walked over to the blacksmith, who was hammering a horseshoe glowing yellow hot.

"Good evening, mister," George greeted the huge, muscled blacksmith. "We're looking for the marshal who owns the black-spotted saddle horse. Do you know where we can find him?"

The blacksmith looked quizzically at both marshals with their badges prominently displayed on their chests.

"Howdy, marshals," the man, who had black smudges on his face and clothes, greeted them. "Are you sure you got the right horse?"

"Well, yeah. I don't see any other black-spotted saddle horses in the corral," Eddie replied.

"Well, that there filly was brought here by three men whose horses are also in the corral. None of them was wearin' a marshal's badge, and if you ask me, they look too ornery to be lawmen."

Eddie and George raised their eyebrows and looked at each other.

"Mind if we take a look at the horse?" Eddie asked. "We may have been mistaken."

"Sure, help yerself," the blacksmith replied as he resumed hammering the horseshoe.

Eddie and George picked their way through the herd of horses until they got to Betsy. She recognized them immediately and greeted them with a nuzzle.

"Hi, Betsy," George said as he stroked her snout. "I knew it was you."

George went over and checked the left flank.

"It's Betsy alright. There's an SS brand on her," George exclaimed.

"Something ain't right about this," Eddie remarked.

"I'll second that motion," George agreed.

They walked back to the blacksmith.

"Excuse us, mister," Eddie said, interrupting the blacksmith's hammering. "Where's the saddle for that horse being kept?"

"Oh, it ain't here," the blacksmith answered. "Those men asked me where they could sell an extra saddle they no longer need, and I told them to take it to the saddle shop down the street." The blacksmith pointed in the direction of the shop.

"Thanks. Much obliged," George said as he and Eddie marched straight to the saddle shop.

They arrived as the proprietor flipped the "open" sign on the door's window to "closed". He saw the men with their shiny badges walking toward the door. He swung the door open and greeted them.

"Howdy, marshals. Is there something I can do for you before I close up for the day?"

"Howdy. We're lookin' for a dark-brown saddle sold to you recently by three men," Eddie declared.

"Why, yes, I know the saddle. It's that one right there," he said, pointing to a recently cleaned saddle on display.

Eddie and George went over and looked at it.

"It's Ben's all right," Eddie said, checking the stirrup and the etchings along the edge.

"No question," replied George.

"It's a nice saddle, ain't it?" the man tendered. "A little worn but nice designs on the fringe and obviously made out of high-quality but tough leather. I can part with it for say…thirty-five dollars, if you're interested. I can even go down a few bucks to…."

The way both marshals stared back in glum silence arrested his sales pitch. He recoiled, bracing himself for some bad news.

"Something wrong?" the proprietor asked suspiciously.

"Do you know where the men who sold you this saddle might be?" Eddie asked.

"Well, I don't rightly know," he responded nervously. "But if I were to guess I would say they're at the Last Chance Saloon at the other end of town. After I bought the saddle, they asked where the nearest saloon was, so I told them about the Last Chance."

Eddie and George looked at each other with the same conclusion and resolve.

The proprietor was obviously worried. "Listen, I don't know what's going on, but I swear I never saw those men before. They wanted thirty bucks for the saddle, but I offered twenty-five, and they took it. Look, I'm an honest man. What's goin' on with this saddle?"

"Look, mister," George exclaimed, "that saddle is stolen property."

"You don't say," responded the proprietor, concerned about the implication of receiving stolen goods.

"It belongs to a fellow marshal," Eddie explained. "Kindly take it off the rack and save it somewhere until we get to the bottom of this."

"From what you just said, you're not in any trouble," George assured him. "Just put the saddle away someplace safe."

"I'll do just that, marshal," he eagerly replie,d clearly relieved. "I'll lock it up in the back room, I will."

"Can you tell us what these men looked like? Is there something that stands out that would identify them?" Eddie asked.

"Well, that's easy. One of the men has a noticeable scar on his left cheek. I felt embarrassed because I couldn't help staring at it."

"What about the other two?" George asked.

"Uh, one broad-shouldered man had a light-brown hat with this large black feather—I've never seen a feather that big—and another shorter man had this bright red bandana—you couldn't miss him in the dark, even if you tried.

Other than that, I didn't take notice of anything else. Sorry I can't be of more help."

"Thanks. Much obliged," George said as they marched out of the store in search of the saloon.

*    *    *

"Whoopee, you won again!" the highwayman with the noticeable scar on his left cheek shouted in excitement at his partner, who wore a tan hat with a large black feather.

The man with the black feather in his hat had been playing at the dice table with ten of the twenty-five dollars they got for Ben's saddle. His winnings were approaching thirty dollars.

The robber with the red bandana was at the bar, on his third glass of whiskey.

The smoke-filled saloon was crowded. A man played lively tunes on a tinny piano. Bar maids served drinks, cavorted with the male patrons, and took them upstairs for ephemeral pleasures. One drunken fool in the corner was singing some obscene ditty with his arms outstretched and a bottle of whiskey in each hand. Another red-faced inebriate kept laughing uncontrollably at unintelligible jokes he never finished telling. The room reeked of alcohol, tobacco smoke, and repugnant human smells.

Eddie and George entered through the double saloon doors and took their stations on opposite sides of the doors. The sheen from their polished six-point star badges caught everyone's attention. Within seconds, absolute silence rolled from the front door to the opposite end of the saloon. Everyone stopped what they were doing. Even the bargirls and their patrons who were going upstairs or coming downstairs froze on the stairway. All eyes focused on the two deputies.

"We're looking for the three men who stabled Marshal Ben Corrigan's black-spotted saddle horse and sold his saddle," Eddie declared. "We want to know the whereabouts of the marshal."

Eddie and George scanned the room and picked out the three men with the distinctive features described by the proprietor of the saddle shop.

"You with the black feather the size of a windmill spoke," Eddie called out to the man next to the dice table. "Turn around with your hands up. The same goes for you, mister, with the knife slash across your face."

"And you at the bar with the bandana that looks like it's on fire, put your hands up and walk towards us," George ordered.

107

As the man with the black feather turned to face the marshals, Eddie caught the quick movement of the man next to him with the prominent scar on his left cheek going for his holstered gun. In one quick, smooth motion, Eddie drew his gun and shot him before he even raised the pistol. The man fell backward, dropping his gun, and laid on his back motionless.

There were screams as everyone dropped to the floor. The man with the giant black feather lost his hat as he dove under the dice table. He managed to fire one round high at the marshals before George and Eddie brought him down in a fusillade of bullets.

All this time, the man with the blazing red bandana held his hands high as if he were trying to reach the ceiling. He stared at the marshals, wide-eyed and speechless.

"You're under arrest," George shouted as he pointed his smoking pistol at the remaining highwayman. "What have you done to Marshal Corrigan, you dirty skunk?"

"George," Eddie cautioned. "Don't shoot him, 'cuz he's giving himself up, and more importantly, he's the only one left that can tell us what happened to Ben."

# Chapter 20

Ben opened his eyes and ears. A clean-shaven man in a brown robe helped him up to a sitting position and gave him water from a gourd fashioned as a dipper. It must have been late afternoon because the sun was no longer overhead.

"Take it easy. ... Don't drink so fast. ... There's plenty more. ... You don't have to hurry," the man said in a comforting voice.

When Ben had drained the last drop, the man refilled the gourd. Ben eagerly grabbed it from the man's hands and drank it empty. As he handed the gourd back to the man, he looked into his face and thought he recognized him from a distant past. Ben could have been mistaken, so he said nothing.

"Fell into a den of thieves did you?" the man asked as Ben rubbed his head.

The water started to revitalize Ben. The buzzing was still there, and so was the pain around the wound. But the disorientation was disappearing.

"I guess you could say I was a mite bit careless," he said as he studied the man's brown robe, tied at the waist with a cord. The robe had a hood, and the man wore sandals.

"Are you by any chance hungry?"

"I could stand a bite," Ben replied, searching his muddled brain, trying to recollect who this man was. The man's oval face, with its dimpled cheeks, had a kindness in it. He had a prominent nose and tousled gray-streaked hair. But it was the tranquil blue eyes that caught Ben's attention. They projected an inner peace that reached out to anyone who gazed into the man's face.

The man went to his horse and brought back some hard cheese and black bread. Ben ate slowly between large gulps of water. The man checked the back of Ben's head.

"Ow," Ben yelled when the man pressed on the most tender part of the bump.

"It's a good thing the Lord blessed you with a hard head," the man said, "since it appears someone hit you with that large piece of wood." He gestured at a three-foot piece of wood, at least six inches in diameter, lying at Ben's feet. "You're lucky to be alive, marshal."

"Well, at least they didn't use a slug from a .45. Otherwise, you'd be burying me, not feeding me."

"By the way, what's your name?" he asked, hoping it would give him a clue. "I'm Ben Corrigan, territorial U.S. marshal, as you guessed from my badge— one of the few things they didn't steal, besides my belt, my clothes, and my teeth. I can't believe they even took my boots."

"The Marshal Ben Corrigan," the monk winced in surprise, "who the newspapers say killed the outlaw Frank Jameson?"

"Yes, I confess," Ben admitted, "—although I don't mean that I'm confessing a sin. I'm the one who got him."

The friar paused with a faraway look in his eyes. Then he caught himself and cleared his throat.

"I'm Brother Wainwright, a member of the Order of Saint Francis. I was on my way north to visit a parish in Taos. By God's grace, I came upon you."

"Thank you kindly for saving my life," Ben said in gratitude. "Earlier, another man in a robe left me to die. He said it was in punishment for my sins."

"It couldn't have been one of my brethren," Brother Wainwright replied defensively.

"No," Ben assured the friar. "His robe was snow white, like his hair. He was crazy, all right. Even though I was delirious, I could see it in his eyes."

"Sounds more like a black angel of death to me," the friar suggested.

"For sure," Ben agreed while rubbing his forehead. "He was the devil in white. Kind of like a wolf in sheep's clothing. By the way, do I know you? Your face looks familiar."

"I can't rightly say, although you look familiar to me, too," the friar said thoughtfully.

"You wouldn't happen to know a Father Bonaventura, would you?"

"No," the friar replied. "Is he a brother Franciscan?"

"I don't think so. He wore a different kind of a robe—gray."

"Well, we're all brothers in Christ, no matter how you look at it. Now, let's get you to Española. We'll find a doctor and a place for you to rest."

The friar helped Ben stand. He led him to his horse.

"I'm sorry to put you to all this trouble," Ben said, wobbly on his bootless feet in thick socks.

"It's the good that I can do in the Lord's name. He rewards everyone who does the least for his brethren. Now, let me help you get on the horse."

Ben mounted a large dark-chestnut gelding, unsure whether he should protest. The friar sensed Ben's reluctance to ride while he would be on foot.

"We're only a few miles from town," the friar said cheerfully. "Anyway I need to stretch my legs."

"Really?" Ben asked, not convinced.

"Really," the friar explained. "I often get off my horse on long trips and walk for a few miles."

Ben smiled back and acquiesced to the generous offer—knowing that he couldn't walk anyway.

The trip took about an hour in the afternoon sunshine. Ben told the friar the events leading up to his being waylaid. Brother Wainwright listened with interest, making occasional polite replies and comments. To Ben's surprise, the stocky friar walked a steady pace and did not need to stop to rest once. As the town came into view, Ben realized the friar hadn't divulged any information about himself.

"Friar, I've been doing all the talking. Can you tell me something about yourself? Maybe that will help me to remember where I saw you."

"Well, there's not much to tell," the friar responded. "I grew up on a farm in western Kansas. Wandered about the West from Seattle to El Paso, doing odd jobs and getting into occasional trouble."

"How did you end up becoming a friar?" Ben inquired with interest.

"Met a Franciscan named Brother Salazar when I was broke and sought shelter at the monastery in El Paso. He introduced me to the communal life. I liked what I saw, stayed to work in their fields, learned what it is to become a disciple of Christ, decided that's what I wanted to do, converted, and became a Franciscan."

"It can't be that simple," Ben commented.

"Well, it wasn't," the Friar laughed. "I just left out the colorful details in between."

Ben winced in pain as his head throbbed when he laughed. He was no closer to remembering when he had last seen the friar. He was certain, though, that it was before the man donned the brown robe.

\*   \*   \*

"This man needs a room and medical attention," the friar said to the swarthy Mexican desk clerk.

*"Este hombre necesita una habitación y la atención médica,"* he repeated in Spanish.

The raven-haired desk clerk with a thick moustache curiously stared at Ben. He half-heard what Brother Wainwright had said. Earlier, the disheveled marshal had tried to explain who he was to the desk clerk, but the man looked at Ben with skepticism, despite the shiny badge. The friar tried to intercede but got the same sorry results.

Brother Wainwright decided he needed to go to the next level and asked to speak to the innkeeper.

*"Me gustaría hablar con el posadero favor,"* he said, hoping for a more receptive audience.

"I'm the innkeeper, and I understood what you and this man said. I speak perfect English," the man said with an accent.

"Then you must understand that this man is not a vagrant," the friar explained. "He's a New Mexico territorial marshal. He's Marshal Ben Corrigan, who was attacked by bandits, stripped of his possessions, and left to die. He needs a place to stay and a doctor to look at his head wound."

*"Santo Hermano* (Holy Brother)," the innkeeper replied in Spanish to avoid being understood by Ben. *"Aceptaré este hombre como huésped cuando dos de mis clientes, quienes también son jefes de policía, pueden verificar quien es él.* (I'll accept this man as a guest when two of my other guests who are also marshals can verify who he is.)"

*"No es mi palabra como un hombre de la tela suficiente?* (Is not my word as a man of the cloth sufficient?)" the friar asked, obviously upset.

The innkeeper looked down and paused. He then turned the hotel register to face Ben and handed him a new-fangled fountain pen.

*"Gracias en nombre de Cristo* (thank you in the name of Christ)," the friar said in appreciation.

*"Usted es bienvenido en el nombre de Cristo* (you are welcome in the name of Christ)," replied the innkeeper.

"It seems you have company," the friar said as Ben signed the register. "The innkeeper says there are two other marshals staying here."

"There is?" Ben exclaimed. "Can you tell me who they are?"

The innkeeper grabbed the register and went back a few pages. "Marshals Eddie Blake and George Whitmore," he replied.

"Great day in the morning," Ben said as he exhaled slowly. "These are my two junior marshals."

"I'd like two night's stay up front, Marshal," the innkeeper requested.

"I obviously don't have any money with me. Marshals Blake and Whitmore can vouch for me. If they don't have enough money between them, I'll telegraph the territorial office. They can forward you the money from Santa Fe."

The man's face once again soured.

"How much is that?" asked the friar.

"At three dollars a night that will be a total of six dollars," the innkeeper replied.

"I'll…I'll offer to pay," the friar volunteered, "with the stipulation that the Territory of New Mexico reimburse me. This isn't my money. I'm sworn into a life of poverty. It's out of the donations for the mission school I was taking to Taos."

"Those thieves were wasting their time holding me up," Ben exclaimed. "Aren't you afraid of getting robbed?"

"I trust not only in divine protection, but also in the reputation of poverty my brotherhood is known for."

"That's still taking a pretty tall chance," Ben replied. "They may not know that."

"I've been blessed thus far," the friar smirked.

"You're in room twenty-six, upstairs and to your left," the innkeeper said as he handed Ben the key and Brother Wainwright handed him the six dollars.

"Now, what about a doctor?" the Friar asked. "Someone needs to check the marshal's head."

"I'd say from here his head looks basically okay," said Eddie, entering the inn with George. "It's on his shoulders right where it belongs. What do you think, George?"

"Yeah, I agree. But he probably has a bad case of cold feet," George replied, looking down at Ben's bootless feet.

# *Chapter 21*

"What's that you say?" the sheriff of Millbrook asked incredulously. "She may have intentionally murdered Svendsen? For what purpose, may I ask? To get control of the bank?"

"I haven't thought about that being a motive," Winkelman replied. "But now that you mention it, that's another possibility."

The elderly sheriff, Ray Dowdy, looked at him with distrust from beneath a Stetson ten-gallon hat that was raised above his tall forehead. He had his arms crossed and his bulldog face grimaced in defiance and disbelief as he leaned back in his chair. Sheriff Dowdy had been an itinerant lawyer, taking legal cases for years all over the territory before settling down as Millbrook's top law officer. He listened to Winkelman's yarn with astonishment.

"It's another possibility," he repeated.

"Poppycock," the sheriff shot back. "Nobody's going to believe Rachel Langford planned to kill Svendsen to get control of the bank. Show me the proof."

"I'm not saying that's so," Winkelman said defensively. "I'm thinking along the lines that she may have done it for other personal reasons."

"Like what?"

"Say to deal with coercion."

"Say what?"

"We all know Svendsen was sweet on her and really miffed when she snubbed him for Corrigan," Winkelman explained, nervously studying the dubious reaction written all over the sheriff's face. "Svendsen may have pressed his case to demand that she drop Corrigan in favor of him. He could have mentioned it during what started as another romantic interlude the night he was killed. She may have decided to rid herself of Svendsen before he could actively interfere with her romance with Corrigan."

"What an amazing story. Excuse me, but I need to use the right word that fits this unfounded mischief: BULLSHIT."

"Between you and me," Winkelman continued unabashed, dramatically looking both ways for prying ears that didn't exist in the empty office. Even the jail cells were empty, and the only sounds in the dimly lit office were their voices. Winkelman narrowed his eyes and whispered, "I talked to the two tarts upstairs at Gentleman Jim's who Svendsen favored. They're all shook up and claim that Svendsen, the night before he was killed, told them of his plan to confront the Widow Langford with his demand that she choose him over the *boms,* as he put it."

"So, you've been at it again have you? Secretly frequenting the cathouse with some of the other of Millbrook's so-called "pious elite". Only it's not so secret. You know you're gonna loose points using their testimony over Rachel's…character." The sheriff tripped over the word "character" as her well-known liaison with Ben entered his head.

Fred knowingly smiled in haughty satisfaction. The sheriff, on his own, had stated Rachel's obvious vulnerability. This discussion was proceeding just as he hoped it would.

"No one's going to believe that," the sheriff insisted, trying to recover. "Everyone that knows her knows she hasn't got a mean bone in her body. She's totally incapable of anything approaching premeditated murder or any heinous crime. She's a pillar of the community. You have an uphill battle on that one."

"Who knows what one is capable of if they're pushed to their limit?" the emboldened lawyer continued. "You know that. You've seen that before. She may have been pushed too far and felt she had to protect her relationship with Corrigan. She's met with Svendsen many times before. There are suspicions that she was having an affair with him from the very beginning, and it continued when Corrigan wasn't around. I'm not saying she's a woman of loose *character,* but her open love affair with Corrigan is a well-known fact."

The sheriff sat silent, weighing every word.

"There's at least a chance, as far flung as it may be, that she may have taken matters in her own hands in a reckless moment," Winkelman continued. "Someone who doesn't know her *character* may bring this up at the territorial prosecutor's office."

"How so? And who would put that idea into the prosecutor's head?"

"If Svendsen made his demand, who's to say that she didn't react in blind rage and panic," Winkelman continued, undeterred. "It's happened before in other places. If she had the perfect opportunity while he was in a compromising, and shall we say vulnerable, position…? There are the right ingredients for the eventual outcome, planned or unplanned.

"I don't believe it, and neither will anybody else. It's hopelessly circumstantial."

"You don't think someone at the prosecutor's office might not bring…."

"What's in it for you, Fred?"

Caught by surprise, Winkelman broke eye contact and looked down at the desk between him and the sheriff.

"You know your past pursuit of the Widow Langford is another well-known fact around these parts. If it wasn't for our respect and concern for Maggie and your wonderful kids, you wouldn't be a welcome individual in our honest community."

"Sheriff, that doesn't have anything to do...."

"She scorned you again, didn't she? Thought you could take Svendsen's place as the prime suitor, did you? Or is it the loss of control over the bank? You want to be president, don't you? And she opposes you. Now, like the vulture you are, you can't wait to swoop in and feed on the carcass. Only you're being thwarted by the Widow Langford, who, like most of us, can't stand you. It's time for you to get her out of the way, isn't it?"

"I thought I could find an impartial ear to hear what may be damaging evidence against Rachel Langford, you being a respected former attorney. I can tell you care nothing for objective jurisprudence. I see I was wrong in coming here to discuss how to proceed with the possibility of a murder in our decent town."

"Do you really think I would arrest her? On pure speculation by someone who has a selfish vested interest...in removing an obstacle to his chance to grab more influence, power, and financial gain...in the middle of someone's tragedy when they're at their lowest ebb. Shame on you. You're a worthless weasel!"

Winkelman grabbed his hat and marched out the front door, slamming it shut.

"I want to see if you have the nerve to bring up charges," the sheriff called after him. "Or are you going to have one of your lawyer cronies at the territorial prosecutor's office do it for you? You coward! You bastard!"

# Chapter 22

"I'm so glad to see you two that I just can't find the words to express myself," Ben said.

"We caught up with your bushwhackers," George exclaimed. "Two of them are on their way to a place where they'll never ambush again, and it ain't the penitentiary. The other one confessed the whole thing. He's locked up, and lucky my gun didn't accidently go off and send him to the same place the other two went."

"We were on our way to find you," Eddie explained. "We stopped at the inn to collect our ponchos. It looks like a storm is heading this way."

"By the way, who's this padre you're with?" asked George.

"Oh, pardon me," Ben turned and grabbed the arm of the venerable brother and pulled him out front. "This is Brother Wainwright, the only one who bothered to haul my half-dead carcass from the brush. If it hadn't been for him, by this time, the vultures and coyotes would be picking at my bones."

"Through God's good grace," the friar humbly replied, "I happened upon Marshal Ben."

"Pleased to make your acquaintance, Brother Wainwright," replied Eddie, vigorously shaking the friar's hand.

"Yes, thank you for rescuing our friend, Padre—I mean, Brother Wainwright," added George, shaking his hand in turn.

"Even though he's blessed with a hard head," the friar cautioned, "he needs to find a doctor to check his head wound."

"See, Ben," the always jocular George responded, "we're not the only ones that tell you you're hard-headed."

"I would never have guessed," added Eddie, "that being hard-headed was a blessing."

"Don't encourage them," Ben said to the friar as they all took a welcome break from the rigors of reality to laugh. Even the innkeeper joined in.

"Ow," groaned Ben, grabbing his forehead. "I do have to find that doctor. My head still aches something awful."

"Dr. Ivan Morales," interrupted the innkeeper. "He's a few doors north. He's got a big sign posted out front. *Él es mi primo y un buen médico.* (He is my cousin and one good doctor.)"

"Good," Ben replied, gently touching the bump on his head. "All I need now are my horse and my duds."

With a smirk, George took the sack he was carrying off his shoulder and extended it to Ben. It contained everything the bandits had stripped off Ben, including his new hat, coveted gun belt, trusty pistol, and prize boots.

"Your horse is in the corral," Eddie chimed in. "And we know where your saddle is."

Ben spent the rest of the evening getting squared away. He had the *un buen médico* examine and bandage his head and repaid Brother Wainwright with money he borrowed from Eddie and George. They treated the good friar to dinner at the town's only diner, where everyone caught up with the incidents that had brought them together. Afterward, fatigue and weariness overtook Ben. He retired to his room.

Ben had a fitful night between his sore head and the urgency of getting back to Rachel. The raging thunderstorm that rolled in and lasted until daybreak exacerbated his restless mood. When he did doze off on the stiff bed, surreal dreams of Rachel wringing her hands in anguish plagued him. Then there were the images of Frank Jameson's lifeless body where he had fallen. Even though he was dead, the outlaw turned his dirty, grotesque face, lifeless eyes blazing, at his slayer. Ben woke with a start, breathing heavily and with a knot in his chest. When he calmed himself and drifted back asleep, the torment would reoccur. The vicious cycle repeated itself throughout the night.

Brother Wainwright remained with them overnight at the inn. The next day at daybreak, before he left for Taos, he knocked on Ben's door. The storm had passed over, and the morning was cloudless.

Ben was already up. He had poured water into the wash basin, dipped his kerchief in the water, and was wiping his face, avoiding the bandage wrapped around his forehead, when he heard the knock.

"Good morning, Friar," he said when he opened the door. "Up so soon?"

"Yes, I'm a day behind, and I'm anxious to get to Taos. May I come in?"

"Please do," Ben replied, opening the door wide. As the friar entered, Ben suddenly realized where he had previously met the friar. Slowly, he closed the door and turned to face the friar, who was standing in the middle of the sparsely furnished room.

"I...I know who you are," Ben exclaimed with wonder. "You're one of the two young bucks that rescued me from a brawl when I first came to Santa Fe to apply to be a marshal. You checked on me before you took off ahead of the law. That's almost forty years ago."

"Yes," the monk replied. "I realized, last night, that's where I remember meeting you. But you had a lot more hair back then, and your face isn't as swollen as it was when I checked to see if you were still alive. That's probably what threw me off."

"Why did you two rescue me from being beaten to death? You took a mighty tall chance defending me from all those tanked-up miners," Ben said, looking for an explanation of something that had puzzled him since the brawl.

"Let's say we had a snoot full ourselves. We were in the saloon across the street, feeling ornery, and when we heard the commotion outside, we took the opportunity to blow off some steam. Mind you, we took your side because we didn't think it was a fair fight."

Ben grinned, thankful they chose to help him for whatever reason.

"What ever happened to your friend?" Ben asked.

The friar shook his head and a sudden sadness swept over his countenance.

Ben took notice and looked at him with anticipation.

"We were two rowdies who happened to fall in together for a short time. We were fired-up drifters, up to the colorful no good I left out of our conversation. Back then, he looked after me and I looked after him. We actually became quite close until we had a disagreement over the same wayward woman. I lost track of him until recently. Came to find out that he never mended his ways. He never had the blessing to ignite whatever good was buried deep in his lost soul. His evil became his undoing."

"I'm sorry. But what did happen to him?" Ben persisted.

"The law caught up with him," the friar said as he stared directly into Ben's eyes. "And he, *Frank Jameson*, was finally put to rest so that he could no longer commit acts of injustice and wickedness."

Ben's mouth gaped open in surprise. He felt lightheaded. Everything hit him at once. He recounted his brash rescue by a younger feisty Brother Wainwright and, of all people, *Frank Jameson*. He recalled his deliverance from despair and depravation by Father Bonaventura. He heard the scream of Jameson as he stumbled out of the thicket and collapsed in a cloud of dust. He felt the anguish of the towns that Jameson and his gang had terrorized.

"May God forgive him," the friar continued, "for the sins he created out of his ignorance and a dissolute life. You see, Ben, you and I were fortunate during our lifetime. We made the most out of our lives with the blessings we were given at the times we desperately needed them. He, for whatever reason, never had those blessings."

Ben didn't move. He was still overwhelmed. "Who would've guessed this could've happened," he exclaimed, clearly moved.

"There's an almighty reason for everything." The friar laid his hand on Ben's shoulder and said, "We must pray for the soul of Frank Jameson, that God's infinite mercy will rescue him from eternal damnation."

Ben was speechless, still awed by the weight of the revelation. Then Brother Wainwright performed the sign over him that Father Bonaventura had performed on that pivotal day in Santa Fe. He moved his right hand vertically and then horizontally, speaking words in that same unfamiliar language that sounded like Spanish, but it wasn't Spanish.

The peace Ben felt rendered him immobile. He was suspended in its serenity.

"Good bye, Marshal," the friar said in parting. "May God go with you." Ben heard the door close. For several minutes he remained standing, stationary with his eyes closed, not wanting to leave this state of absolute tranquility. Then there was another knock at the door.

"Hey, Ben," Eddie called out. "It's us. You ready for breakfast before we move out?"

# *Chapter 23*

"We've got to tell her," Veronica said to Grace as she pushed her mother's wheelchair to a stop in front of Rachel's house.

It was a stifling hot afternoon. The sun peeked between billowing white cotton-ball clouds that rolled across the deep-blue sky. Impatiently, they waited under their sun bonnets for Millie to arrive so they could get out of the intense sunlight and get on to warning Rachel of the rumor that was brewing.

"That Winkelman is a bad apple like that whoremonger Svendsen," Veronica's mother declared.

"Please, Mama," Veronica replied. "We know how bad he is. The point is, how do we tell Rachel about the gossip spreading around town when she's in such a terrible state?"

"I'll tell her," Grace offered. "I know how to break the news. Anyway, it's only hearsay. I doubt it's that serious. You know how people chitter-chatter: Somebody twists her finger in the morning, and by sundown everybody's talking about how that person broke her arm. I'll tell her."

"We'll all tell her," the newly arrived Millie chimed in. "We're her closest friends. We need to stand together to show our solid support if the rumor is indeed true."

"You know," Grace observed. "I don't see her. She's usually sitting in the front parlor gazing out the window of late. I don't see anyone in the parlor through the open window."

"Yeah," said Veronica wrinkling her brow and staring into the open-curtained parlor window. "She usually does her errands in the morning and spends the rest of her day at home."

"Oh, she's probably in the kitchen," Millie replied, "making herself something to eat."

"Or maybe taking a siesta in her bed in this heat," replied Grace. "I know I would."

"Or maybe visiting the privy," Cornelia added.

"Well, let's get to it girls," Millie said, leading the group to the front door.

With apprehension, the band of supporters marched up the walkway. Millie knocked, and they waited for a reply that never came. Millie knocked again and called to Rachel, announcing their arrival.

Still no answer.

"Oh, my," Veronica uttered apprehensively.

"Well, I guess she's just not home," said Grace, ignoring Veronica's hint of an ill omen.

Millie twisted the door handle and discovered that it wasn't locked.

"She must be somewhere close by if her door is unlocked," Millie said as she looked at the others. Veronica had a trace of worry written on her face that she couldn't hide. Grace and Cornelia had the blank expressions of a wasted visit.

Millie opened the door to let them in. She wanted to put to rest any notion that something might be amiss. They filed into the parlor.

"Rachel, honey, it's us. We came to call on you," Millie called out.

No one replied.

"I'll check her bedroom," Grace volunteered. "She's probably *dead* asleep in this heat."

Veronica jumped at the word "dead".

"Okay," sighed Millie, shaking her head. "We'll check the kitchen. Come on Veronica and Cornelia."

"Somebody check the privy," Cornelia shouted. "She may be out in the privy."

They entered the tidy kitchen and what caught their attention was a small pile of mushrooms atop a piece of cloth in the center of the kitchen table.

"Oh, my God," Veronica gasped and then covered her mouth with her hand. "Those look like the Destroying Angel."

"She's not in her bedroom," Grace announced as she walked into the kitchen. She saw the look of fright on Veronica's face and the concern on Millie's. Cornelia was rolling her eyes in disbelief.

"Them mushrooms ain't the Destroying Angel," Cornelia argued.

"What's going on here?" demanded Grace.

"They are too," Veronica insisted. "Look at the light-brown spots on their caps. Rachel's done poisoned herself."

"What?" shouted Grace. "I don't believe it."

"Now, Veronica," cautioned Millie. "Let's not get carried away."

"I knew it was too much for her," shouted Veronica. "It's too much for anybody to endure. Oh, God!"

"You know what?" Grace exclaimed. "They do have the panther spots on the cap. They look like the Destroying Angel. We gotta find Rachel," she screamed. "It doesn't take long for it to take its effect."

"I'm telling ya," Cornelia protested. "They ain't the Destroying Angel."

"This has gone far enough," Millie yelled. "Would you all please settle down."

"The stable out back...the stable," Grace cried out. "We forgot to look in the stable!"

"Why ain't nobody checkin' the privy?" Cornelia complained. "She may be out in the privy."

Just then the back door opened, and Rachel entered the kitchen, smiled at them, closed the door, and started to unfasten the ribbon of her sun bonnet.

"What in tarnation is going on here?" Rachel asked innocently.

The room went quiet as everyone stared, open-mouthed in relief, except Cornelia.

"Mmmpf, told ya they ain't the Destroying Angel," Cornelia chortled.

"We thought...that is, Veronica thought," replied Millie, "you might've intentionally done something terrible by eating those mushrooms that look like uh, the Destroying Angel."

"What?" Rachel shouted as she glanced at the mushrooms and then each one of the women.

"Oh, my God," Grace sighed. "How did we come to believe you would do that? We should have known better."

Veronica caught Grace's glare and blushed with embarrassment.

Rachel smirked as she walked over to the peg mounted on the wall by the back door and hung her sun bonnet.

"Where were you?" Millie asked nonchalantly. "We, uh, knocked on the door but, uh, you didn't answer."

"Oh, I was in the privy."

"Mmmpf," grinned a vindicated Cornelia. "Told ya so."

"By the way," Rachel explained. "Those mushrooms I bought from Barney at the general store. They're the good-eating button type. I wanted to make mushroom soup tonight."

Veronica stared at the pile of mushrooms with her hand back over her mouth. She wondered what possessed her to start thinking ghastly thoughts.

"Veronica, are you okay?" Rachel asked, noticing the red cast to Veronica's face. "You look flustered."

"Um...uh...well, yes, I'm fine. Thank you."

"Let me guess," Rachel deduced. "You all thought I did myself in because, adding to my other woes, there's word going around town that Fred Winkelman wants to bring murder charges against me."

Grace joined Veronica in blushing crimson. Millie looked up at the ceiling and shook her head. Cornelia chuckled.

"Why would I leave my friends in such a state?" Rachel asked. "Why would I leave my family in such a state? Why would I insult God in such a state?"

"Who told you?" Millie asked, not bothering to respond to Rachel's rhetorical questions. "I mean who told you about Winkelman's outrageous claim?"

"Barney and his wife told me," Rachel exclaimed. "Besides you, my dear friends, I'm happy to say I have other friends in town."

"What are you going to do?" asked Grace.

"He'll leave me no choice," Rachel replied. "If he decides to press charges, I'll hire the best lawyer in Santa Fe or even hire a high-powered attorney from Denver or St. Louis or back East."

Rachel looked at them with a faint smile and heaved a sigh.

"Don't worry, my dear," Cornelia said in a raspy voice. "Nobody in this town is going to let him get away with this. Nobody likes that highfalutin' dandy. We'll all be behind ya."

"Mama's right," added Veronica. "The whole town will never back him. He's a disgusting ne'er-do-well who should be run out of town. He probably would be if it weren't for Maggie and the children."

"You're mighty lucky to have two smart grown sons," Millie said. "They'll settle the score with this scabby lawyer. Why, just wait till Ben hears of this."

Rachel threw another faint smile at them, went to a knife rack on the kitchen counter, grabbed a chopping knife and a cutting board, went to the pile of mushrooms, and started dicing them.

"Now, who wants to stay for some 'Destroying Angel' mushroom soup?" she asked, tongue in cheek.

\*   \*   \*

"Ma, what do you want us to do? Nothin'?" an enraged George asked, standing next to his equally incensed brother. "You want us to stand aside and let this crooked lawyer accuse you of murdering that whoremonger of a bank president because you were greedy?"

Rachel sighed and looked at both her sons with sympathy and understanding. They were in the parlor. Her sons were sweaty from their hard ride from their ranches. Both had the heat of anger etched on their faces. She stood next to them and placed a hand on each of their shoulders.

"You boys make me proud, and I love you for trying to protect me. But roughing up Fred Winkelman isn't the answer. It's only going to make things worse. It's not worth getting both of you in trouble with the law. Everyone knows his selfish motives. I'll get a good lawyer to defend me. He'll never win. You'll see."

"We gotta do somethin'," Harry responded, his fists clenched in anger. "He ain't gonna get away with this. Someone needs to knock him off his perch."

George shouted, "That's right. We're not gonna stand by and allow him to...."

"Think of your families," she cautioned. "What would it be like for them to be missing their husbands and fathers when you're stuck in prison? Fred's an attorney. He'll set the full measure of the law on you like a duck on a June bug."

George took a deep breath and exhaled slowly. His eyes narrowed in quiet rage. Harry unclenched his fists, angry tears filling his eyes.

Rachel turned and faced the window, observing the town's daily routine with renewed longing.

"I yearn to get my life back to the happiness I had before your father died," she said dreamily. "Those were the good days. I could smell the blossoms in the garden, and their scent would paste a smile on my face that would last the whole livelong day. How I enjoyed hearing you boys laughing and playing, taking as much delight in a hoop and a stick as your children do now. I miss how your father made me feel so special each and every day. It was such a wonderful time in my life."

She paused, caught herself, wiped her eye, and stated, "And it won't happen again unless we do this thing right. There's been enough violence and killing in these parts over the last few months. We don't need to add to it. We're supposed to be decent folk. It's time to let the law take its course."

She swirled around and confidently exclaimed, "Sheriff Dowdy says Fred hasn't got a chance. He says he knows several good lawyers that would be more than happy to defend me in Santa Fe. He even says he's considering dusting off his old law books to represent me. I can't see how Fred can win this thing. He's going to be so embarrassed."

Her sons glanced at each other in mutual agreement to acquiesce and then looked at Rachel.

"Okay, Ma," said George, "if that's the way you want it."

"That's the way it needs to be if we're going to live respectfully in this community."

Then they hugged each other.

Harry added, "But if the law doesn't do you justice, we're not gonna guarantee that Mr. Fred Winkelman doesn't escape our justice."

"Ow," Harry shouted as his mother twisted his ear.

# *Chapter 24*

"Those country bumpkins aren't going to insult me. I'll show them," Fred Winkelman vowed as he threw another shirt into his carpetbag. The bag bulged with the clothes and other items he was going to take on his trip to Santa Fe to meet Horace Newman, the territory's top prosecutor. It was just before daybreak, and he had to catch the train that left town shortly after six o'clock.

His beautiful wife, Maggie, watched him with dismay from the doorway to the bedroom on the second story of their modest, but well-furnished, frame house near the edge of town. She was reaching the breaking point. Throughout their marriage, she had struggled to cope with Fred's seamy philandering side, his bouts of abusive drunkenness, and his preoccupation with avarice at the expense of their family. Fred ignored his wife and children, except when he needed something or could use them to his advantage. On more than one occasion, he had treated them as expendable when they got in his way. When he would apologetically crawl back to her in defeat, she forgave him only for the sake of her children.

Despite these adversities, she had persevered in raising three bright, young, and well-mannered children. Outwardly, she and her children lived the comfortable, idyllic family life expected from the town's only attorney. Behind the scenes, she was miserable, lonely, and disappointed with her lot in life, with the exception of her cherished son and two daughters, all under the age of ten.

This latest attempt by Fred to grab power and wealth in this obscure, meaningless, windblown town at her family's expense became the catalyst for her to disengage and depart.

"Fred, who insulted you?" she asked.

"You can't be that much of a simpleton," Fred exclaimed, unnerved by her question. "Rachel Langford and her backward sons to be specific. I offered to make her a director of the bank. She acted like I insulted her. Can you imagine that? It's probably because she's insulted that she wasn't offered the bank's presidency. I always knew she was a greedy bitch."

Maggie frowned at Fred's crude name calling of her friend, Rachel, and the preposterous accusation of Rachel being greedy.

"I can tell by her response," he continued with his rant, "that she and her brood are probably going to block my effort to be the bank's president. And I'm supposed to take this sitting down? Well, I've got the goods on her. She'll rue the day she crossed me."

"Did she turn down your renewed advances toward her?" Maggie pointedly asked.

"What advances? What are you talking about?"

"You know what I mean," she sneered.

"I already apologized for that mistake. How many more times are you going to nail me to the cross for that one?" he snapped back. "You don't hear me bringing up the ranchers that made eyes at you at the Fourth of July dance do you? You danced with every one of them."

"You're the only one making something out of nothing," she shot back. "I've never given you cause to be jealous like you have given me."

He leveled a steely-eyed glare at her. She recoiled and fear welled in her chest. He dropped what he was doing and made the first move to approach her with his hand raised to strike.

"Mama, I can't sleep," her youngest child, Thomas, interrupted. The altercation with his parents had awakened him, and he rolled out of bed and ran to her, rubbing the sleep from his eyes. "Are you and Papa having another fight?"

Fred stopped and lowered his hand and glowered at both of them.

"No, we're just having a discussion," she said as she hugged him. "Now go back to bed. It's too early for you to be up. You don't want to be sleepy at school."

"Okay, good night, Mama," he said.

"Good night, dear," his mother replied.

"Good night, Papa," he said as he trundled back to his bedroom.

Fred didn't answer his son but went back to packing his bag.

"We're leaving you," she said calmly. "I'm taking the children with me to my parents in Kansas City."

Fred didn't answer her. He forced himself to smile and acted unconcerned as he grabbed more clothes.

"I'm serious," she continued. "I...we can't take your abuse any longer. You have no feelings for us, and it's plain you never will. I'm not going to go on pretending that I'm your loving wife."

"Maggie," he replied with disdain, "you don't mean that. You and the kids never had it so good. Why, there's dozens of women in this town that would change places with you."

"Then the dozens of women you cavorted with can, but I'm taking my children."

He stopped and took a sideways glance at her.

"When you get back from Santa Fe, we won't be here," she flatly stated.

"You'll be back," he assured her. "Two weeks living in squalor with your nagging mother and drunken father will sober you up. I'll bet it won't take you that long to come to your senses. Then it'll be your turn to come crawling back to me. Only I may not take you back. So you might want to reconsider."

"We're not coming back. We're never coming back."

Fred put on the brown hat that matched his brown suit, grinned, picked up his carpetbag, and walked past her, rudely brushing her aside. He stepped down the stairs, grabbed the doorknob, and flashed an arrogant smile at her before leaving.

His brash reaction was all that she needed to harden her resolve. She felt relief and determination surging in her. The picture Fred painted about her family in Kansas City was true enough. What he had neglected to mention was the contempt her parents had for him and the genuine love of family they had for her and their grandchildren—something his cold heart didn't.

Stoically, she turned, went to her son's bedroom, and peeked affectionately at him slumbering peacefully. Then she went to her daughters' bedroom. They were both asleep, but the eldest stirred and opened her eyes, not fully awake.

"Mama, is everything all right between you and Papa?" she asked dreamily.

"Yes, my child," Maggie replied as she sat on the bed next to her. She kissed her on the forehead and gave her a big hug. "From now on everything is going to be okay. You, me, your sister, and your brother are going to live with Grandpa and Grandma. Papa is to stay here. How would you like that?"

Her daughter's eyes grew wide, and she smiled. "I would like that a lot. They really love us."

# *Chapter 25*

"Welcome, Mr. Winkelman," the New Mexico Territory's principal prosecutor, Horace Newman, greeted Millbrook's only lawyer to his plush legal office in Santa Fe. It was located near the old Spanish governor's hacienda.

Fred thought he had mistakenly entered a chamber in a royal palace. Never had he seen a legal office so elegant. From the open tall, narrow windows, he could hear songbirds as sunshine poured in, bathing the room in its golden radiance. The windows were surrounded by open curtains of royal blue with yellow trim and gold tassels. Shiny brass oil lamps were equally spaced around the room's perimeter. They accentuated the walls of smooth, white stucco, on which hung various paintings of the New Mexico countryside. Thick and cushy light-brown carpets littered the floor of large, shiny beige tiles. Wooden furniture was stained dark in such way as to expose the natural beauty in the grain. The cushions of dark red looked sumptuous on the different chairs and rich leather couch. The room was filled with the fragrance of fresh wild flowers in colorful glass vases that were scattered about the room. All this was topped by a domed ceiling decorated with one-inch tiles of white and turquoise.

He had made the one-day trip from Millbrook by train and arrived on the date the territory's top legal attorney said he was available to meet with him. The trip taxed Winkelman's patience and rump, which was sore from the hard seat on the train. He was anxious to get an audience with the man who would be instrumental in promoting his case in the charge of the murder of Kristoffer Svendsen by Rachel Langford.

"Thank you, Mr. Newman," he said as he shook the short, stocky man's hand, still in awe of the surroundings. "I'm glad we finally have a chance to meet."

"Please be seated," Horace gestured to a luxurious red-velvet chair in front of his dark-walnut desk. "Would you care for a cigar?"

"Oh, no thank you. I don't smoke."

"Well, if you don't mind, I'd like to light one up," Horace said as he lit a thick, dark cigar. "It helps me think more clearly."

"I don't mind at all," replied Fred as the aromatic smoke drifted toward him, making his eyes water. He gave a couple of light coughs.

"I read your complaint," Horace continued. "It's…quite an interesting charge you level at the accused. She claims it was self-defense to prevent her from being physically violated. … You claim there's reasonable evidence that this was an opportunistic homicide to prevent her attacker from actively interfering with her romantic relationship with another. ... The victim was the prominent owner of the only bank in town." He smiled at Winkelman, looking for confirmation. "I think I got that right."

"Yes, indeed," Winkelman eagerly affirmed. "It's quite complicated, but I think there's evidence to suggest that she lured him into a compromising position to murder him to prevent him from openly interfering with her other, more serious, relationship."

Horace took a long puff from the cigar, exhaled the smoke toward Winkelman, placed the cigar in a red-marble ash tray, steepled his hands, and sighed, looking down at his desk.

"I have the testimony from two women that Kristoffer Svendsen confided in the night before he was killed," Winkelman said as he blinked away the irritation from the smoke while pulling out some papers from his briefcase. "They claim he told them he was going to make a demand to Rachel Langford to drop her relationship with...."

"Marshal Ben Corrigan," answered Horace.

"Ah...yes. You are familiar with Rachel Langford's relationship with the Marshal?"

"I'm somewhat familiar with the Marshal's connection," Horace replied, lightly tapping the fingertips of his steepled hands.

"Then you agree that there's reasonable doubt that Rachel Langford acted totally in self-defense? That she may have acted to protect her relationship with the Marshal at the opportune time?"

"Oh, there's reasonable doubt all right," Horace said as he looked up into Winkelman's arrogant face. "But the dubiousness is in the accusation of Rachel Langford's intent to commit murder."

"How so?" asked a deflated Winkelman as he dropped the papers he was holding onto his lap.

"I have the affidavit from Millbrook's Sheriff Ray Dowdy," Horace touted. "It clearly states that the defendant, Rachel Langford, justifiably killed Kristoffer Svendsen as he attempted to rape her. Sheriff Dowdy, as you know, is a well-known respected former attorney, who could have had a place on the bench if he so desired."

"Well," Winkelman replied, "I for one am not sure it was rape. There's well-founded speculation that she was involved with Kristoffer Svendsen when Marshal Corrigan was out of town. She could have very well...."

"The front of her blouse was torn down to her waist," Horace continued, leaning back in his chair and tapping the armrests. "Her fingers were swollen from her attempts to pummel her attacker. She nearly lost her ripped britches. Witnesses heard her screams from in front of the bank."

Winkelman sat motionless, not sure how to respond.

"This, uh, well-founded speculation has some serious challenges," Horace continued. "I have a signed document with more than fifty signatures from the residents in and around Millbrook testifying to Rachel Langford's outstanding character. Notwithstanding her private personal relationship with Marshal Ben Corrigan, who by the way has a distinguished record for almost forty years enforcing the statutes of the Territory of New Mexico. You know, he retired yesterday from the U.S. Marshals with full honors."

Horace lowered his head and peeked at a fidgeting Winkelman.

"As far as the speculation, people have a right to mind their own personal affairs as long as they're not breaking the law. Isn't that right?"

Winkelman turned his head and stared at the wall.

"Say, even those who choose to privately frequent the upstairs of an establishment called Gentleman Jim's Watering Hole. Mind you, even though word gets out."

Sweat formed on Winkelman's upper lip as his lower lip started to quiver.

"Needless to say," Horace concluded, puffing on his cigar while leaning back in his chair, "I don't see any reason to prosecute this case. Any recently graduated lawyer would decline it in a heartbeat."

"Well, if that's the way you feel, then I suppose there's no need to pursue this any further."

"Go home, Fred," Horace suggested. "Take the shortcut. And the next time you want to see me about another complaint, make sure it's not personally motivated. Otherwise, I'll have you disbarred. Have I made myself clear?"

A red-faced Fred Winkelman grabbed his papers, tossed them in his briefcase, and left without saying a word.

Horace Newman smiled with satisfaction as he leaned back with his hands behind his head, puffing on his cigar. A travesty of justice had been averted. Luckily, the citizens of Millbrook got wind of Fred Winkelman's request for an audience with the territory's top prosecutor. They flooded his office with telegrams and letters in defense of their highly esteemed fellow citizen. It made for interesting reading, putting together not only the speculation of Winkelman's motive, but also his nefarious character.

Horace had no doubt that Winkelman was peeved that Millbrook rallied behind Rachel Langford, and they forewarned him of Winkelman's intent. What also helped was a discussion with Marshal Corrigan, whom he knew and respected. The Marshal was at first shocked, but then corroborated the same positive consensus of Rachel's character. Despite Ben's obvious bias, he spoke objectively of her favored standing in the community, citing her participation in a number of civic and charitable activities.

It took a lot of work to calm Ben down and persuade him not to fulfill his oath to throttle Winkelman. After all, Ben's unblemished career might be tarnished by such a rash act. He assured Ben that he would send the disreputable lawyer and his sham packing to Millbrook in absolute humiliation. If Winkelman felt barely tolerated by the Millbrook community, he was going to be totally ostracized when he returned from his trip to Santa Fe. The punishment the townspeople would exact would be far worse than any thrashing Ben could deliver to Winkelman's tender hide. Who knows? Fred Winkelman may pull up his roots and finally leave town. At the very least, Winkelman would leave Santa Fe without his complaint seeing the light of day and with a stern warning to toe the line.

It was a shame, he thought as he took another puff from his cigar, that Ben retired from the noble body of law officers that needed men of his integrity and stature. Oh, well, after all the venerable Marshal had gone through during the past four decades, he had certainly earned his pension. This last difficult encounter with the outlaw Frank Jameson was probably all the persuasion Ben needed to hang up his badge.

Like Ben's junior deputies, he had urged Ben to wait a few days to fully rest before heading out to Millbrook. But as soon as Ben got his walking papers, he wished everyone he knew a fond farewell and left Santa Fe in the sunshine of early afternoon.

"Gee, I hope he gets his girl," Horace whispered to himself. Then he thought, this would make a sensational dime store novel back East. I wonder if I should take the time to write it? I think I will, when I find out how it ends.

# *Chapter 26*

Thunder rolled across the open country around Millbrook, and lightning lit up the scrubby terrain as the remaining traces of daylight disappeared. A storm had churned its way into the area from the mountains in the west. The black clouds laden with moisture poured down buckets of rain. It was a gully washer. Rivulets carried away the sandy soil and the town's refuse into the countryside. Bleached arroyos filled and became temporary alabaster ponds. The ground that was not underwater became a mushy muck for anything that traveled on it. The wind gusts between the buildings rolled tumbleweed through the deserted streets at the speed of a locomotive at full throttle.

Into the town, down the city's main street plodded the newly retired Marshal on his black-spotted saddle horse. Both horse and rider were sopping wet, weary, and aching for dry shelter.

Ben squinted through the sheets of rain, searching in the fading light for Rachel's home. When he got there, he stopped Betsy and paused in the downpour, wondering whether he would receive a warm welcome or any kind of a greeting. She never replied to any of his telegrams from Santa Fe. For all he knew, Rachel could be involved with somebody else, or she had decided to move on alone from their tenuous love affair. Steady streams of water dripped from the brim of his hat, and the wind drove the drips into his face.

A flash of lightning followed by a loud peal of thunder urged him off his horse. He tied her to a hitching post out front, stroked her muzzle in gratitude, and traipsed up to the front door. The curtains in the parlor had not been drawn. A light flickered from a back room into the parlor. Otherwise, the house was completely dark. Fearing disappointment, he hesitated when he reached her door, but the overriding desire to know where he stood took hold. He knocked. The light grew brighter through the window as Rachel carried the lamp to the door.

"Yes, who are you? What do you want?" he heard her sweet but apprehensive voice ask. It was a melody he hadn't heard in months.

"Rachel, it's me, Ben," he said, voice quavering.

Only the rushing of the wind and the pounding rain broke the silence. He grabbed the crown of his hat before it blew off his head with one hand and pushed down on his billowing poncho with the other.

When the wind gust subsided, Ben knocked again on the door. "Rachel, I…I came to talk to you. Please let me in."

Her muffled whimpering penetrated through the door. Then he made his bold statement.

"Rachel, I've come to marry you. If you don't open the door, then I'll know that you've moved on. I'll understand."

The whimpering became crying as Ben leaned heavily against the drenched door in the relentless driving rain to get as close as possible to Rachel's aura on the other side.

Her crying grew louder amid the rumbling thunder. The intensity of the wind increased, and the downpour became heavier. Ben concluded that Rachel couldn't open the door because she had indeed moved on. He pressed the open palm of his right hand on the soaked door in an effort to reach her—to touch her in parting.

"Goodbye, Rachel. Wherever you go, may God go with you. I understand, darlin'," he said in a soft voice as tears welled up in his eyes.

Ben gasped, turned, and started walking back to Betsy, who had her head down in the heavy torrent. Then the front door swung open. Ben turned around and saw Rachel running to him.

"Oh Ben…Ben…Ben," she cried as she embraced him in her wet nightgown and bare feet. "Don't go. … I love you. … Don't go."

He wrapped his poncho around her, and they kissed oblivious to the fury around them.

"I'll never leave you again, darlin'," Ben promised. "From now on, we move on together."